Carly's Buck

Chet's handsome, Carly thought. He had her favorite combination of blue eyes and dark hair, and he looked about her age, thirteen. Only he didn't appear to be too glad to see her. "Shhh," he said and looked back at the deer he'd been watching beyond a tangle of bushes.

Carly is glad to focus her attention on the buck also; studying the magnificent creature helps her forget her troubles, at least for a while. Carly's mother has recently died after a long battle with cancer, and Carly can't forgive her father for being distant during her mother's last months. Wanting to get away from him, Carly has come East to stay with her aunt and uncle in the Adirondacks. But the move hasn't solved her problems. She doesn't fit in with the kids in her new school, and Chet's indifference is frustrating.

Carly persists in making friends with Chet, though, and as she gains his trust, she discovers a poetic spirit beneath his awkwardness. She also learns that hunting animals like the deer is an everyday part of his life. This angers Carly as much as her father's behavior did, and she devises a plan to protect her beloved buck. Only when a tragic accident occurs does Carly acknowledge that she herself is not without guilt.

Readers will relate to Carly's conflict as she slowly resolves her idealism and learns to accept people for who they are.

CARLY'S BUCK

Other novels by C.S. Adler

Kiss the Clown
Shadows on Little Reef Bay
Get Lost, Little Brother
The Evidence That Wasn't There
The Cat That Was Left Behind

C.S. Adler

CARLY'S BUCK

CLARION BOOKS

TICKNOR & FIELDS: A HOUGHTON MIFFLIN COMPANY

NEW YORK

Clarion Books
Ticknor & Fields, a Houghton Mifflin Company
Copyright © 1987 by C.S. Adler

Library of Congress Cataloging-in-Publication Data
Adler, C. S. (Carole S.)
Carly's buck.
Summary: In dealing with her mother's death, Carly
befriends a wild deer over the opposition of her
friend, an ardent hunter.
[1. Death—Fiction. 2. Deer—Fiction. 3. Hunting—
Fiction] I. Title.
PZ7.A26145Car 1987   [Fic]   86-17183
ISBN 0-89919-480-X

P   10   9   8   7   6   5   4   3   2   1

To Helen Edelman, my talented young friend,
for a happily ever after life.

With thanks to Paul Cullen,
who speedily provided
the reading material I needed
on whitetail deer.

1

Carly hadn't heard a single bird or seen a squirrel on her hike into the mossy woods around her aunt and uncle's house. Then smack in the middle of nowhere, she came upon the boy crouched on a platform up in a tree. He didn't seem aware of her. "Hi, up there," she said softly, to keep from startling him. "What are you doing?"

He jerked to his feet and stared down at her silently. Handsome, she thought. He had her favorite combination of blue eyes and dark hair, and he looked about her age, thirteen. Only he didn't appear too glad to see her.

"Shhhh," he said and looked back at whatever he'd been watching beyond a tangle of bushes that screened Carly's view.

"Can I climb up and look too?" she whispered.

He frowned at her, then grudgingly signaled her to come. Agilely, she climbed the crosspieces nailed to the big oak's trunk. She'd come out to the woods to escape

1

the purple pain which had started throbbing like one big bruise inside her chest again. While she hadn't expected to find anything that would help amidst the sameness of brooding greenery, she'd been desperate enough to try anything.

Being alone for big chunks of time had worsened the sorrow that Carly had nicknamed the purple pain. She needed people. She'd always made friends easily. The trouble was the population of this isolated town in the wild Adirondack Mountains of upstate New York seemed to be mostly cows, or else barking dogs that protected their homes fiercely. A family with sons was supposed to live in the house half a mile down the county road from her aunt and uncle's A-frame. Carly hoped this boy was one of the sons.

He was crouched watching again when Carly hoisted herself onto the platform next to him. She looked where he was looking.

"I don't see anything," she said after a minute. The afternoon sun had turned the dark August leaves to an incandescent green-gold in the clearing which was framed on one side by a snarl of bushes and on the other by the inevitable dense evergreen trees.

"Keep talking and they'll disappear," he said. His voice rumbled deep as a man's.

She scanned the sun-streaked clearing again and whispered, "Well, if I knew what I was looking for, maybe I could see it."

He pointed with a hand too large for his bony arm, and suddenly she saw the doe in the shadows. Carly caught her breath in delight. The doe's reddish brown fur blended with the brown of bark and branch and earth, but even better was the camouflage of her fawns lying motionless a few feet away from her.

The doe stood alert, her large ears and liquid dark eyes trained in their direction. Carly concentrated on being still, as still as the deer, as still as the boy. For the first time since she'd arrived a week ago, she forgot her loss. The magical beauty of the deer lighted the oppressive dark green of the Adirondacks for her. It was like glimpsing the princess in the hulking castle.

The doe lowered her head to crop some weeds. Her body melded into the surroundings as she lay down in a shadier spot. One of the fawns stood up on bamboo legs. It suddenly jumped stiffly over the spotted back of its twin and turned around as if inviting the twin to play. Carly laughed out loud. Instantly the doe was on her feet. She snorted and her white tail disappeared into the far side of the thicket. Carly didn't see the fawns go, but suddenly the clearing was empty, really empty this time.

"That did it," the boy said, slumping to the platform. He pulled a canteen from his pocket and took a swallow from it.

"I couldn't help myself," Carly said. "The fawn was so cute."

He grimaced at the word and she defended herself. "Well, seeing wild deer like that in the woods, that's a beautiful experience. Thanks for sharing it with me."

"That's okay," he said. "It's no big deal."

"It was to me."

He didn't respond. She offered, "I'm Carly Alinsky. I'm staying with my aunt and uncle, Lu and Ben Weibel. Who are you?"

"Chet Graham."

Right, she remembered, that was the name of the neighboring family. "Is this Graham property then?" Carly asked, tapping her foot on the platform.

"Uh-huh."

Getting him to talk was a challenge. She surveyed his long lanky figure from big creased work boots to broad shoulders topped by a head as small and graceful in its way as the deers'. "I didn't know I was trespassing," Carly said, chatting her way to a subject that would open him up. She looked doubtfully down through the trees toward the rock face, huge and smooth as an elephant's hide, which she'd scrambled over to get to this patch of woods. "I didn't see any fences."

He grinned. "The only boundary marker around here is maybe a blaze mark on a tree, or a rusty metal stake with rocks and nettles hiding it."

"Then I guess I can't be blamed for trespassing," she said and smiled.

"You're the kid from California," he stated.

"So you've heard about me?"

4

"It's not that big of a town," he said. "The local news comes free if you buy your bread and milk from the lady at the convenience store."

Carly knew the place he meant. It was plunked across the highway from the little white church with the outsized steeple. Rolling fields and rocky pasture on either side of it stretched to the green bristled heads of the nearest mountains.

"All I know about *you* is there are five Graham boys," Carly said. "Which one are you?"

"The youngest."

"Are you all so tall?" She had meant to compliment him, but the question made him look at his feet as if he were embarrassed.

Quickly she changed the subject. "Will they come back?"

"The deer?"

She nodded.

"Not till after sundown maybe, maybe not at all if you really made the doe nervous. Being nervous keeps her and her fawns alive. That snort she gave? That was her warning to hide. Deer are geniuses at hiding. You can be standing ten feet away from them and not see them."

She guessed by the length of his answer that she'd found the right subject and asked, "But they'll come back eventually?"

"Maybe. Whitetails are unpredictable. That's another way they stay alive."

"Did you build this tree house here to watch them?"

"It's not a *tree* house; it's a deer stand. My brothers built it. . . . Usually, some part of the day, the deer come to that clearing. Yeah."

"Where else do they go?"

"Oh, they've got their places. I don't know all of them. Where the food is, like pastures in the summer. They'll graze right out in the open, and they get into the old orchard in the fall when the apples are ripe. If you look, you can find deer trails all over the woods, regular routes they travel to get to water or bedding places or food supplies."

"You know a lot about deer."

"I know some, yeah. Don't you have whitetail where you come from?"

She laughed. "The only wild animals who survive the Los Angeles freeways are human. Where I live, everything's built up. I've never wandered around in woods like these—except when my father and I went camping in the mountains." A pang reminded her. The subject of parents was open wound area. "Listen," she said. "Is it okay if I come here sometimes? Just to watch. I won't bother them."

He shrugged and hesitated. He was a private person and felt possessive about those deer, she guessed. Grudgingly he said, "So long as you're careful not to spook them again." When he stood up, he towered over her. His biceps bulged below the sleeves of his shapeless

6

T-shirt, but most of him was thin, as if he hadn't properly grown into his body yet. She bet his face was prettier than hers with those intense blue eyes and thick black lashes. She hoped he liked the way *she* looked. "My little chipmunk," her father used to call her because she was perky and quick and small.

"Tell me more about the deer, Chet," Carly begged.

"I've got to go," he said.

"Some other time?"

"Sure." He was in such a hurry to escape her that he jumped from midway down the crosspieces of the makeshift ladder and took off at a run.

Cute, she thought and grinned because *cute* wasn't a word he'd like applied to himself any more than to the deer.

Another minute alone and the purple pain ballooned again. Carly pressed her knuckles to her chest to keep it from bursting. She'd be sore when the pain subsided. Lu thought the pain was simple grief over her mother's death, but Carly knew it had to do with her father too. Anger was in it. She couldn't forgive the way he'd behaved, her father whom she'd adored.

"Of course, when I lost my parents I was older than you," Lu had said cheerfully when they'd sat down to talk the evening after Carly arrived. "I was a freshman in college, and being away from home and with so much else to think about, it was probably easier for me. I do remember bursting into tears in the middle of a class once. Everyone stared and I died of embarrassment. . . . They say it's better to let go and cry it out. You're supposed to get over it faster that way."

"But it doesn't get better," Carly had tried to explain. "It's awful and thick and purple and it chokes me."

"Purple?" Aunt Lu had questioned.

"Purple, like red is excitement and yellow is joy and purple is pain."

"What an imagination!" Lu had said and patted Carly's cheek. "Just believe me, you'll stop hurting eventually."

Carly hoped Lu was right but doubted the pain would ever stop. It frightened her that she couldn't control it. She couldn't fend it off, and she couldn't get rid of it when it came. Maybe it was punishment. But if she was going to be punished, her father should be too. She'd never been as good a daughter as her mother deserved, but he'd failed even worse as a husband.

One of these days Carly would tell Lu the truth about the older brother she admired so much. Maybe Lu could explain why he'd neglected his sick wife in the months before she died. Lu was a fair-minded person—a listener. The listening had been what Carly had liked best about the aunt she'd only gotten to know well a year ago when Lu and Ben stayed with them on a West Coast vacation. "You have such a good relationship with your father," Lu had said then. "And I can see why. He's a terrific guy."

That was last year, but just a few weeks ago, Carly had told her father, "I hate you so much I may kill myself if I have to stay here in the same house with you." He'd turned white, big ruddy man that he was, beefy with muscles from working out in the gym three times a week and sailing in races every weekend he could get away from his record business. He'd turned white and stopped objecting to Carly's going East to live with his sister for a while.

As long as she could remember, Carly had known she had power over her father. She could make him wince and hurt when no one and nothing else could. "She's my girl," he told people proudly. "Chip off the old block." Not that she looked like him. She didn't at all. She looked like her mother, who'd been wiry and dark-haired with enormous doe-like eyes that were the last thing still alive in her as her body wasted away those last months in the hospital.

But Carly had the same energy her father had and she was strong for her size. Most important to him, she wasn't afraid of anything physical. She'd hike way out on a heeling sailboat in rough water. She'd laugh, sitting beside him in the small plane he sometimes rented to get in flight hours for his pilot's license if he missed the landing field and had to circle and try again. He liked to do things hard and fast and so did his daughter.

Mother had been such a timid woman. She'd huddled in the cockpit of the little sailboat out of the spray, trying not to cry out as the boat bucked and slammed down on the wave tops. While Carly had ridden down the freeways behind her father on his motorcycle, screaming with joy as he wove recklessly through the traffic, Mother had never donned the helmet he'd bought her, never ridden the motorcycle at all. But she had been a loving wife and mother. And when the cancer began eating up her body, she'd been brave then. Her father had been wicked to fail her.

A blue jay shrieked as it landed on a nearby branch. Carly wondered who it was scolding. Then she saw the gray squirrel. The tip of its tail flicked out and refolded along its back. Jay and squirrel stared at each other until the jay flew off the branch noisily. The squirrel continued running along its roadway until it leaped through space to another branch on the next tree. A puddle of darkness filled the clearing where the deer had been. The milky sky was fading into evening and Carly was feeling all right again.

Time to go home before she ended up getting lost in the dusky woods that stretched between the Weibels' ten acres and the Grahams' land. Did Chet like her, Carly wondered. What kind of a boyfriend would he make? She'd had a boyfriend just before Mother got sick, but dropped him to spend her free hours with Mother. Chet was probably shy, but Carly could get around that. He'd talked well about the deer. And those deer—it was magic that they'd appeared to lift her spirits, like symbols of hope. She'd come back to find them again soon.

She climbed out of the tree and slid back down over the rocks the way she'd come up. The rocks here were strange. Rubbed smooth, they had tufts of grass and weeds growing in their cracks and scales of a greenish gray lichen mottling their gray backs. Carly followed the stream back to the little redwood A-frame that was overpowered by an enormous woodpile on one side and huge trees on the other. Not another house in sight. Her aunt and uncle liked it that way, but Carly had been afraid she'd made a bad mistake when she saw the place for the first time last week. Its isolation gave her the shudders.

The bottom half of the landscape was full of the tallowy light of late afternoon as she passed the wagon wheel marking the entrance to the driveway. Lu and Ben's car meant they were home from the Environmental Education Center where they taught, set up exhibits, and maintained the trails. Carly bounced into the living room exuberantly. The room was furnished, in order of importance, with books, a wood stove, floor cushions, flip-out couches and area rugs. A narrow iron staircase rose to the sleeping loft which was partitioned into two bedrooms. Near the staircase was a fireplace. The kitchen was separated from the living room by a counter and the bathroom.

"Guess what I found in the woods," Carly called out.

"Something good?" Lu asked, pushing her long black hair behind her shoulders as she stood at the kitchen sink cleaning carrots for dinner.

"Fantastic," Carly said. She hugged her chunky young aunt. "A mother deer and her fawns in living color."

"That is good," Lu said.

"Chet Graham showed them to me."

"Oh, you met Chet? He could end up in your eighth grade class this fall. Quiet, isn't he?"

"He can talk."

Aunt Lu laughed. "I should have known nobody could be quiet around you."

"Do you think I talk too much?" Carly asked.

"Not for me, you don't."

"Why don't you ask *me* that question?" Ben said. A toilet was flushing in the bathroom he'd just left.

"Because you'd say yes," Carly said. "You wouldn't have picked Lu if you liked females who chatter."

"Shrewd observation," Ben said and sniffed. He was a slim, bald-headed young man with a beard and small regular features. Carly suspected he hadn't been too happy to have her come to live with them. It had taken him aback to learn she planned to attend school here in the fall. She wasn't sure whether he objected more to having his privacy invaded or to her personally. Whatever, she hoped to win him over eventually.

"Ben, did you hear me telling Lu about the deer?"

"Hard not to hear things in this little house," he said.

"Well, do you think I could tame them?"

"Don't even consider it. Come hunting season, it wouldn't be too healthy for those deer to have lost their fear of people."

"When's hunting season?"

"Mid-November around here."

"Ummm. Well, nobody's going to shoot my deer, I'll tell you that."

"Your deer?" Ben said. "I thought you saw wild animals in the woods."

"Well, they're mine in a way."

"What way is that?" Lu asked indulgently.

"Because they're special to me, they're mine," Carly said.

Lu gave her a one armed hug, still holding the carrot peeler. "You nut," she said.

"I think you're cute too," Carly told her.

She chattered about the woods during dinner, deliberately keeping it light. People liked having you around better when you acted cheerful and kept your miseries to yourself. She'd have her deep talk with Lu some other day.

2

Carly woke up exhausted from wrestling with bad dreams all night. As always, the dreams scuttled out of sight before she could face them down in the cheerful light of morning.

She could smell coffee and hear the radio news broadcast, which meant that Lu and Ben were getting ready for work. Her impulse was to hide out under the covers until they'd left, but she had already learned that if she didn't get up and give them her early bird chirp, one of them would be sure to come up and worry over her. They were only in their late twenties. She'd expected them to take their parental role more casually and not interfere with the independence she was used to. Her mother and father had treated her like a mini-adult for as far back as she could remember.

Sighing, Carly rolled out of bed, pulled on shorts and a T-shirt, and ran downstairs. She gave Lu and Ben a cheeful "Hi" as she joined them at the long wooden kitchen table Ben was proud of having made himself.

"Sleep okay?" Ben asked. Above his neat brown beard, his narrow eyes studied her intently.

"Oh, sure," Carly answered. She poured herself a glass of juice from the bottle in the refrigerator.

"Sounded as if you were thrashing around a lot."

"Did I wake you up, Ben? I'm sorry," Carly said.

"You cried out in your sleep a few times," Lu said gently.

"Did I? I must have been dreaming." Out of the corner of her eye, Carly saw them exchange a meaningful glance. They'd been talking about her, her broad-hipped aunt with the beautiful eyes and hair, and her wary uncle. She didn't want them deciding she was too depressed or too disturbed by her mother's death for them to handle and shipping her home to her father. Even though she wasn't hungry, she put a piece of bread in the toaster. Not eating would be one more bad sign to them.

"How about coming to the Center with us? You can help me work on that new exhibit," Ben said.

"No, thanks." Carly was airy. "I'll just rest and read today. Next week school starts and then I'll be busy enough." The Environmental Education Center was okay, but right after she'd arrived, Ben had set her to work typing labels for him there. Hours of one-fingered label typing was not her idea of summer vacation fun.

"It's amazing you don't get bored here alone all day," Lu said.

15

"There's plenty to do around here if she wants to keep busy," Ben said. He looked meaningfully at the bookshelves in the living room. He'd already mentioned that the books piled haphazardly on the shelves needed to be organized and dusted.

Carly hated housework, but she didn't want to give Ben cause to dislike her; so she said nothing. As far as she was concerned, the dishes could pile up to the roof and spiders could build cobweb cities on the bookshelves. If she suggested he and Lu use part of the extra money her father was sending for her keep to hire a cleaning lady, she wondered how Ben would react. Not well, probably. Ben was the kind of person who valued any kind of work for its own sake.

"Keeping busy keeps you healthy," he'd told her the first night she'd come. One of his many maxims. Well, it wasn't one of hers. She did favors for people to show she liked them, not out of obligation.

"I guess you haven't had much time to yourself in the past year, have you, Carly?" Lu asked sympathetically.

"No," Carly said. She had told Lu about her efforts to keep her mother company, to stay with her so that Mother wouldn't be alone.

"Nothing like sitting around thinking to get you down though," Ben said.

Usually Lu suffered his truisms in silence, but on this one she called him. "Gets *you* down, you mean," Lu said. Her smile took the edge off her words. "Come on, Ben. We have to stop for gas, don't we?"

"I'll fill the bird feeders, Ben," Carly offered to placate him. There were three bird feeders around the yard, a small one near the kitchen window where the nuthatches and chickadees and titmice came, a larger one for cardinals and blue jays and squirrels, and the hummingbird feeder near the hammock.

"Fine, and then maybe you could get at—" Ben began, but was cut short by Lu.

"You just relax and do what you please, Carly. Anything you want from the supermarket? We'll do our food shopping for the week on the way home from work tonight."

"No, I like what you eat." They were vegetarians and ate a lot of tofu and miso soup and bean and corn dishes. Food had never mattered to Carly anyway. Her father, who loved food, had always complained that she ate like a bird.

She kissed them both good-bye. Ben remained stiff as usual, but Lu hugged her. She obviously enjoyed Carly's natural affectionateness.

After they'd gone, Carly relaxed. When she was feeling down, it was easier to be alone. "Nobody needs a sad face around them," Dad used to say if she brought him her woes. He was only glad of her company so long as it was cheerful company. That training served her well with friends. More than one had told her they liked having her around because she was an "up" sort of person.

For a minute she considered Ben. Unless he started liking her, he'd probably begin nudging her out of here soon, and she had no place else to go, except home. She wouldn't give her father that satisfaction. They'd both neglected Mother and taken more in love and services than they'd given to her for years. But Carly, at least, had tried to make it up to her at the end.

"I'm not going to pretend to something I don't feel," her father had answered Carly when she'd taken him to task for staying out late and disappearing weekends with his clients and friends.

"Why not?" she'd asked him. "If it makes her happy, why not?"

"Because I can't," he'd said.

She knew he'd explode if she kept at him, but she did anyway and he'd stormed out on her. Her father did a lot of storming out and burning rubber as he zoomed down the driveway. He was ten years older than Ben, but her dad acted like a teenage boy sometimes. Ben. For all Carly knew, he wasn't so mature either. Hadn't he as much as said he wasn't ready to take on the responsibility for a child yet?

It was last year in California when Dad had bluntly asked his young sister when she planned to start a family. Lu had put him off by telling him, "Someday maybe."

"I had you pegged for the maternal type," Dad had said. "I wasn't around much when you were growing up, but I do remember you had a roomful of dolls you fussed with all the time."

Ben had thrust himself into the conversation then by saying decisively, "We're in no rush to take on the responsibility of kids."

Did Ben feel responsible for Carly? Probably. And he hadn't had much choice about letting her come. A week after the funeral Carly had called Lu long distance and said, "I've just got to get away from here or I'll go crazy. Please, Lu, I won't be a bother."

"But what about your father? He must need you badly now," Lu had said.

"He understands. He says if you'll take me in, he'll let me go." He'd also said wistfully that he'd miss Carly and that he hoped she'd want to come back soon, but she didn't tell Lu that. If Lu didn't take her, there were cousins from Mother's side, but they were conventional people who'd treat a thirteen-year-old like a child and fence her in with rules and regulations. Carly could go to a boarding school, sure, but that would limit her freedom of choice even more.

Impulsively, without consulting her husband, Lu had finally said, "Well, of course, you're welcome to live with us for a while. So long as your father says it's okay."

Taking the welcome as open-ended, Carly had promptly gone about getting the proper signatures on her school-record transfer. She had almost relented when Dad had said, "Do you really think it's necessary to go to these lengths to punish me, Carly? You're going to miss me too, you know."

"No, I won't," she'd lied, though her heart flip-flopped and she'd had to be mean to keep from giving in. "I don't need you the way that mother did."

"Your mother accepted the bad along with the good in me. She was satisfied."

"Not at the end she wasn't."

Dad had flinched and the purple pain had zapped Carly hard. After that he hadn't said much, just driven her to the airport and accepted the kiss good-bye she'd given him before she boarded her plane.

Now here she was, and here she planned to stay, maybe even through high school. If worse came to worse, she would even dust a book or two to get on Ben's good side.

She wondered if Chet Graham had a big loving family. Considering all the kisses she had in her, she wished she'd had one instead of being an only child. Her mother had been affectionate—until the end when she hurt so much she didn't want to be touched. "Blow me a kiss, darling," Mother would ask Carly at the end of her daily after-camp visits that long last month in the hospital.

They all blended into one despairing blur in Carly's mind now, the afternoons during the spring when she'd sat beside the bed at home or in the hospital. She'd held her mother's hand and rattled on as fast as she could go about the things that had happened in school and some things that hadn't that she made up just to see her mother smile.

". . . And my science teacher changed the D to an A because I explained to him how you could look at the question from a totally different point of view and come up with the answer I gave. He said I was an original thinker, Mom. Nice?"

Even though she'd known her mother didn't care anymore about the complications of Carly's friends' lives, Carly had kept her informed of all new and imagined developments just to have something to fill the awful silence of that painful dying.

"Dad says he'll try to come tonight," Carly would tell her, lying to give Mother something to look forward to. That was in the hospital, when he came rarely and then only stayed for a few minutes.

"He's got to entertain those TV people from New York. He needs the big contract, you know," Carly would alibi for him when he slunk out too soon.

"I know," Mother would say. She had complained neither about his absences nor his brief visits. Sometimes she cried quietly, but she wouldn't tell Carly what she was crying about.

"Are you in pain? What is it? Is it about Dad?"

Silence, a weak smile, and a weaker, "I'm all right, darling."

When Dad did appear on an evening when Carly wasn't there, Mother never failed to tell Carly he'd come.

"It's so hard for him. He hates sickness," Mother said repeatedly, excusing him to Carly as Carly excused him to her.

Carly hated sickness too, just as much as he did, but she'd never said that to her mother. And she was a child and he was supposed to be an adult, a big strong man. Oh, how wicked and weak her father had turned out to be! Even if her mother could forgive him for his neglect of her, Carly wouldn't, couldn't, never, never would.

Trying to run away from the purple pain, Carly decided to go see what she could see from the deer stand. Either the deer or Chet would help.

3

C arly took her paperback copy of Tolkien's *Lord of the Rings* with her to the platform in the oak tree. She'd read the book twice before, but she liked reading favorite books over and over. Even now, she'd still go through her aged copies of *The Little Prince* or *The Wind in the Willows* with pleasure on a rainy afternoon. New books were enjoyable or not, but old books were pillow-comfortable.

The morning sun warmed the wooden platform and made her drowsy. August hung heavy as a quilt over her. The clearing was empty. All she could hear was the *pock, pock, pock* of a woodpecker drilling for insects in a dead tree nearby and the leaves' sighing as the breeze fingered them.

On just such a morning she had sat back to back with her father in a rowboat on a high mountain lake, drowsing over her fishing rod. When he'd suddenly begun reeling in his line and pulled the pike on board, he'd given a yell that echoed from the surrounding cliffs.

"You bring me luck, Carly," he'd said then. "I'd rather go camping with you than with anybody else I know."

"Daddy's girl," Mother had called her without envy. Mother had been proud to have produced something that pleased Dad so much. "He's such a powerful man," she said. "He has so much vitality."

"I'm going to be my father's business partner when I grow up," Carly had told an associate of his at a party just before they'd found out Mother had cancer.

Her father had put his head back and laughed heartily. "There's my girl," he said. "Isn't she something?"

"I hate you," she'd told him on the way back from the funeral. "I wish I never had to see you again as long as I live."

"Don't say things like that, Carly," he'd beseeched her. "We need each other more than ever now your mother's gone."

"I don't need you," she'd said. But now she was going to have to prove it.

The warmth of the filtered sunlight and the effects of her sleepless night put her to sleep. When she woke up, a noonday sun was glittering through the leaves directly overhead. If either the deer or Chet had come, she'd missed them. Nothing to eat, and she was hungry. She should have made herself a sandwich, but she'd forgotten. She climbed down, leaving Tolkien on the platform, and went foraging for berries. Chet had said something about the deer liking an apple orchard. She wondered if it was far and which direction it was in. Idly she followed the faint tracing of a path through a gully going, she guessed, through the Grahams' property.

She wasn't looking for the deer anymore; so it surprised her to see one at the bottom of the gully drinking from the slick ribbon of water there. When it lifted its head, she gasped. Antlers, velvet-covered antlers, crowned a deer so slender and well-shaped that the word *dainty* came to her mind. Antlers meant a male deer, a buck. He looked towards her. Entranced, she held absolutely still.

The buck's ears swiveled, one forward and one back, searching for the source of the noise that had alerted him. Finally he lowered his head, took another sip of the stream, thought better of it and bolted. He sailed through the bracken up the far side of the gully in an about-face that would have done credit to an Olympic gymnast. Carly simply had to share what she'd just seen with someone, someone like Chet who would understand. But how was she going to find his house in the woods? Well, she'd try. She didn't have the patience to return home and hike along the road to the Grahams'.

"Helloooo," she called just in case someone was near enough to answer. Mosquitoes found her. She slapped at them and slid down the gully between juniper bushes and rocks and thorny brambles. She crossed the brook where the buck had drunk and followed his hoofprints up the far side, hoping her sense of direction was good enough to keep her from getting lost.

Off to her right, she spied a red dot in a tree. It could only be an apple. She headed that way and found the twisty branched trees of the old orchard Chet had mentioned. The apples were wormy, but she gnawed a few sour mouthfuls to ease her stomach pangs. An abandoned hay wagon stood beside a rutted, grass-grown road and Carly followed it. She kept going downhill, through overgrown fields full of thistles and milkweed and the mullein Ben had identified for her by its thick hairy leaves and yellow flowers. An old barn bulging at the seams and ready to fall down came next.

Then, across an expanse of rough lawn, she saw a white shingled house with a wide front porch and a fat woman sitting on it. A car was parked on the scraggly lawn in front of the house, and beside the road near an enormous vegetable garden stood Chet. He and a man with thick glasses and gray hair were working on a tractor.

Carly was so delighted to have found him that she yelled out, "Chet! Hi. It's me, trespassing again."

Chet saw her but ducked his head without answering. Embarrassed, she guessed.

"Hello, there," the man with him called in a pleasantly deep rumble that sounded like Chet's. "What can we do for you, little lady?"

"I was just walking in the woods and came out here,"

Carly said as she joined them. "I'm Carly Alinsky, the Weibels' niece."

"Well, pleased to meet you. I'm Harry Graham. Appears you've met my son."

"Yes, at the tree house yesterday."

"Tree house?" The amiable Mr. Graham grinned as he peered at her myopically through the thick lenses of his rimless glasses.

"In the woods," Carly said. "The one your sons built."

"She means the deer stand," Chet told his father.

"Oh, yeah. Well, Chet neglected to mention that. He's a pretty closemouthed fellow, my son Chet." The tone of Harry's voice made it sound like a compliment, and he thumped Chet's back approvingly for good measure. They were the same height, but Harry Graham looked twice as massive as his son.

"I just met the father of the fawns we saw yesterday, Chet," Carly said. "He was a beauty. He was drinking from the stream at the bottom of the ravine near the deer stand."

"Small eight pointer?" Chet asked, and when Carly said she guessed so, assuming he was referring to the antlers, he added, "That's not the father. That's last year's fawn. He's only a year and a half old."

"Really? I can't believe it. He looked so perfect!"

"You're lucky," Harry told her. "Most folks'll tramp through the woods for days and never see more than deer tracks, if that."

27

She smiled. It was like a fairy tale when the magical creature appears to the one who needs it most.

"Well," Harry said. "We better get this balky tractor fixed so Chet can mow the grass before it takes over the place. You could go visit with Chet's ma on the porch there, Carly. Gladys likes company and don't get enough of it."

In an instant both Chet and his father had forgotten Carly and were intent on the engine again. "This could be the sucker that's causing the problem, Chet," Mr. Graham said as he pulled up a loose wire. "Whyn't you start her up and we'll see."

Carly drifted over to the porch and introduced herself to Gladys, who greeted her cordially.

"Beautiful day," Carly said.

"Hot," Gladys said. "Takes all my energy just to get up and dressed on a day like this. I can't take the heat. Bad circulation. My legs don't want to go." She looked down at the plump white pillars propped in scuffs beneath her skirt.

"I guess it is hot," Carly said. She hadn't noticed before. "My aunt says you have five sons. Do they all live at home?"

"Just Chet and Joe, but Joe's working down to the supermarket, bagging for the summer. Joe's a worker. Studies hard too. Chet's a good boy, mind you, but not the student his brother Joe is."

"But Joe's older, isn't he? Maybe when Chet gets to high school, he'll become a student."

"Not likely," Gladys said with calm acceptance. "Chet, he likes to get off in the woods, just like his daddy. Him and his daddy are real close."

"Is your husband a farmer?" Carly asked looking at the tractor and the vegetable garden.

Gladys laughed. "A farmer? Oh, my no. Harry's a builder. Built a lot of houses back of the high school there, but now all Harry gets is remodeling work. And most folks around here don't have the money even to hire him for that. Harry jokes he's semiretired, but he don't want to be. . . . You thirsty? Want some water?"

"Yes, please," Carly said.

"Well, go on in the kitchen there. There's glasses on the shelf over the sink. You can bring me one too, if you don't mind."

Was she an invalid, Carly wondered, or did she just like to be waited on? Before Mother had become too weak, she'd always been busy doing something—trying gourmet dishes, puttering in her garden, refinishing antique furniture. Mother had never been content to just sit.

Carly found an ice cube tray in the freezer and put cubes in both the glasses she brought out.

"Nice," Mrs. Graham said, looking as pleased as if ice were something special. "Nothing better than a cold drink of water on a hot day."

"Umm." Carly sat down on the step as the tractor engine revved up and thundered into action.

"That does it," Mr. Graham yelled over the sound.

29

Chet and the tractor disappeared around the back of the house.

"Won't take Chet long if you want to sit awhile and wait. Most of the grass is browned over. No rain to speak of this month," Gladys said.

"Do your older sons live around here?" Carly asked and sipped her water.

"No. One's down in Florida working in his wife's family's business, and one works in a lumber camp out in Oregon. Then we got one in the army."

"Having just two kids at home to take care of must seem easy to you," Carly said.

"There's enough to do, let me tell you. I used to work over to the elementary school. In the cafeteria. But since my legs gave out, I don't go nowhere. Good thing I got the TV to keep me company."

Carly waited for Gladys to ask her questions, but Gladys seemed incurious.

"Harry got an electric bug gimmick last year to take care of the mosquitoes, but I don't think it works good," Gladys said as Carly swatted a mosquito on her arm.

Harry appeared at the porch just then. "You ladies are just too sweet-blooded," he said. He planted a foot on the porch step and rested his hand on his knee. "Mosquitoes don't like the taste of me. Green flies in June though, they're not so fussy."

He sat down on the top step across from Carly and said sympathetically, "Not too many kids out this way for company, are there? You going to be glad when school starts?"

"I usually am," Carly said.

He was the one who asked the questions. Where had she come from? Why had she come?

"I lost my mother this summer," Carly told him. "She had cancer."

"Oh, that's sad," Gladys said as if she meant it.

And Harry said, "Too bad. Hard on a girl. The girls're always closest to their mamas."

"Actually—" Carly began to correct him and then thought better of it. She wasn't about to explain why she had had to get away from her father. "Actually, it's hard on my father too."

"Must be," Harry said. "Don't know what I'd do without Gladys here. A man needs a good woman to keep him warm."

Gladys laughed. "Plenty of me to keep a man warm, but you'd be better off without me, Harry. You're a better cook anyways."

"No, sir. Can't do a pot roast like yours, Gladys. Nobody can."

Gladys chortled. "Want to know the secret of my pot roast?" she asked Carly. "The secret is I burn it a little. Never used to mean to, but I learned to do it on purpose because Harry likes it that way. This man here is so easy to please. Him and Chet. I got lots of complaints but not about my men, let me tell you."

The Grahams sounded as unreal as a TV sitcom family to Carly. Real was her own mother's anxious attempts to please her husband, attempts which always resulted in his finding fault with her. "What's with the sauce? Are you trying to make us all fat?" he'd ask when she tried a new recipe. Or he'd lose something and storm around the house swearing and accusing Mother of having mislaid it.

Her father's good nature had showed only toward Carly. His doting wife had irritated him so much that he'd often made disparaging remarks about her in front of guests. He had given Mother expensive presents for anniversaries and birthdays though, as if presents could make up to her for all the put-downs. "Why do you let him talk to you that way?" Carly had once asked her mother, only to be told that her father didn't mean half of what he said. Mother had been too meek, Carly thought, and for her meekness she had suffered.

"Here's Chet," Gladys said. "Done mowing, son?"

"We're out of gas," Chet said. He looked at his father.

"Okay, you two kids want to come to the gas station with me?"

"Sure," Carly agreed quickly, hoping Chet wouldn't object to her company.

"Bring me back some ice cream, hear?" Gladys called after them as they settled into the front seat of the car with Carly in the middle. "Butter pecan or maybe rocky road if they got it."

32

"I left my book on the deer stand," Carly said as they took off. "I hope I can find my way back there from your house."

"Chet can show you the way," Mr. Graham offered. "You stay and have a sandwich with us, and then Chet can walk you back to the tree after lunch."

"Oh, that's not necessary," Carly said.

"I don't mind," Chet said unexpectedly. "Nothing better to do anyway."

"Sounds like someone else will be glad when school starts up next week," Mr. Graham said. "It's funny with summer vacations. When I was a kid, it was just the same. Never could wait until they began and always glad when they ended. 'Course my daddy kept me hopping with chores all summer."

The conversation on the way to the gas station and back was all between Carly and Chet's father. She wondered that she'd gotten Chet to say anything to her when they were alone on the deer stand yesterday.

Carly wondered even more, after a lunch of ham sandwiches and soda and ice cream, when Chet led her back to the stand without saying a word the whole way.

"Thank you," she told him as they stood under the platform.

"That's okay."

"Your family is very nice."

He nodded, said "See you in school," and took off in as much a hurry to escape as the deer had been.

Aggravating boy, Carly thought. Why couldn't he be friendly? He didn't have anyone else around to talk to as far as she could see. Maybe he didn't like her. Maybe he hated her. She hoped not because she liked him a lot.

She was so intent on Chet that she headed home without retrieving the book she'd gone to the deer stand to find.

4

arly woke up at dawn. The world outside
the window next to her bed looked entic-
ing, all pale and pastel, moist with new-
ness and alive with bird calls. Barefoot, she slipped out
of the house and took off for the woods to get her book.
A cushion of moss squished under her feet. Islands of
mist transformed the ordinary into the mysterious. She
shivered in the chilly air but didn't turn back. It was an
adventure to be out early enough to startle a nibbling
rabbit which froze with a piece of green leaf hanging
foolishly from its mouth.

The quarter of a mile between her aunt's house and
the deer stand disappeared in less time than Carly would
have believed possible, and then she was up in the tree.
No book there, but as she was wondering who could
have taken it, she got a different reward for coming.
The fawns were playing together in the glade. One spread
its front legs and crouched, then bounded awkwardly,

landing some distance from the other. The second fawn lowered its oval head and outsized ears and ran at the first. The jumper skipped sideways, and an exuberant game of chase began around the clearing. Carly watched, enchanted.

She didn't see the mother until all at once the doe was there. The fawns immediately forgot their game and ran to feed. Tears filled Carly's eyes as the fawns confidently tipped their heads up to nurse at their mother's teats. Suddenly, the dainty buck arrived. He stood at some distance from his mother and the fawns, his antlers held proudly erect. The doe snorted at him threateningly, and the buck lowered his head, pretending he was only there to sample the weeds at the edge of the clearing. The fawns finished and curled up on the ground for a snooze. The buck wandered off and soon the doe left too. In the dappled light, the spotted hide of the reddish brown fawns made them hard to see. So did their stillness. Not so much as a flick of an ear gave their positions away.

Carly returned to the house to find Lu and Ben eating breakfast, a kind of rice dough called mochi that puffed up when it was baked. "Can I have some too?" she asked as she pattered into the kitchen.

"I made some for you," Lu said. "Have a nice walk?"

"Incredible." Carly dried her wet feet with a paper towel and sat down at the table. "I saw my whole deer family. They were playing leapfrog in the thicket, and I saw the fawns *nursing*."

"That is amazing," Ben said.

"I mean, I feel so privileged to have seen wild animals like that. It's so special. I can't even express it right."

"You said it very well," Lu told her. She pushed her long hair back from her face and smiled approvingly at Carly. "Listen," she said, "today's supposed to be a scorcher. Ben and I are going for a dip in the lake near the Education Center during our lunch hour. Want to join us?"

Carly was tempted. As she was hesitating over whether to go or stay and track Chet down to continue making friends with him, the phone rang. Ben reached to the wall behind him and answered it. "No, no, we're all up. No problem. In fact she's been out for a walk already. Here, I'll let her tell you about it." He handed the receiver to Carly. "Your father," Ben said.

She was furious. Ben *knew* she didn't want to talk to her father. Last time he'd called, Carly had refused to go to the phone. She took the receiver and said tensely, "Hi, Dad."

"Carly, honey, it's so good to hear your voice. It's four o'clock in the morning here and I've been up all night. Couldn't sleep. How are you doing?"

"Fine."

"Good. Not missing me yet I take it? Well, I'm missing you, kid, and that's what I'm calling about. I've got a business trip to New York next week. How about joining me? We could get tickets for a show."

"I don't think so."

37

"Come on. It'd be fun. We could do up the town together—dinner, theater, museums, whatever you want."

She resented his thinking he could bribe her as if she were a sulky child and he were blameless. "Invite somebody else to play with you, Dad. I'm not your friend anymore."

His voice hardened. "You're my daughter."

"That's not my fault."

"Your mother would be upset if she knew you were acting this way."

Carly lunged across the room to return the receiver to its cradle. How dare Dad try to make her feel guilty by using her own mother against her! She was too angry to cry, but she was shaking when she turned to face her aunt and uncle at the table.

"What's the matter with you?" Ben demanded. "He's your father."

"He wouldn't stay home with her," Carly said between clenched teeth. "He didn't care about her feelings, and I don't care about his."

"I'm sure he cared, Carly," Lu said, "but watching somebody you love die in pain is too hard for some people to bear, especially a strong, healthy person like your father who's always been so physical."

"She needed him and he didn't stay. He had to go to the *gym* and away on his stupid business deals."

"Maybe her suffering scared him," Lu said.

"Then he's a coward. Mother's the one who was scared. He knew how scared she got, and he left her alone."

"She wasn't alone," Lu said. "She had you there."

Carly bowed her head, overwhelmed by the purple pain that was erupting like hot lava inside her. She had been selfish too. She and her father both were to blame for treating Mother badly.

"So what are you going to do, Carly?" Ben asked. "Stay mad at him forever?"

"Maybe," she said.

Ben stood up abruptly and took his dishes to the sink. He turned the water on full force. Carly could feel his dislike. He didn't understand. He thought she was wrong not to forgive her father. But Ben hadn't been there the night her mother broke down and begged her husband to stay, wept and begged him because she was finally so weak with fear that she had no shame left. Carly tossed her head. She couldn't change her convictions to make Ben like her.

"You're the only close family your father has, Carly, and he does love you very much," Lu said.

Carly wondered if he loved her enough so that if *she* were dying in pain he'd stay by her side and endure watching her. Not likely. Maybe he loved her, but he loved himself more.

She waited until she had control of herself again and then said, "Tell me what my father was like when you were kids, Lu."

"Honey, he's so much older than I. He was already in college when I started school. . . . I remember he used to buy me neat presents, and I was always glad to see him come home, but I can't remember ever having a real conversation with him."

"But was he kind and thoughtful?"

"He was very energetic, and he talked fast—like you do, and he had a loud laugh. . . . I'm sorry, I just don't remember."

"Well, he's *not* a kind, thoughtful person. Believe me, he isn't, and I just don't respect him anymore."

"Come on, we're going to be late for work, Lu," Ben said. He sounded angry. "You grab your swim suit and I'll bring the towels."

"Are you coming, Carly?" Lu asked.

"No, thank you." She looked at Ben.

Lu seemed distressed and hesitated, then said, "I'll get my suit," and ran upstairs.

"I'm sorry I make you so mad," Carly said to Ben. "I'd really like you to like me, but I can't change what I feel."

He shook his head, not looking at her. "I just hope I never have a daughter as judgmental as you. I know I'm not perfect, and I'd hope my kid could love me anyway."

His words stung. She did love her father. That's what hurt the most.

After Lu and Ben had gone, Carly curled up in a chair and put on a tape of folk music, a sweet-voiced rendition of ballads including her favorite, "Barbara Allen." Ben was judgmental too, she consoled herself, every bit as much as she was, and furthermore, he didn't know what he was talking about. He would have had to see her mother's eyes light up when she thought she heard her husband's step. He would have had to watch her suffering as Carly had.

*

The missing book made a good excuse for Carly to walk to Chet's house and ask him if he knew anything about it. The woods had quieted down from its dawn awakening. All she heard was her own sandaled feet crunching the leaves and snapping the twigs that littered the ground which went either uphill or down, never level. She paused to peer at patches of pale green lichen and tiny moss trees that looked like miniature landscapes on the rug-sized stone outcroppings. The matchstick-sized, red-headed moss was called British Soldiers, Ben had told her. It was surprising how interesting the woods could be under close examination, and, except for getting lost, Ben said she had nothing much to fear. The rattlers had been so heavily hunted for bounty they were cleared out of these woods, and the other snakes were harmless.

Carly stopped at the stream where she'd seen the buck drinking and caught a tiny frog. She cupped it in her hand and let it tickle her palm, then set it free. The woods soothed her, but Ben was right. Being alone with so much time to think invited the purple pain. As if she could outrun it, she quickened her pace on her way to Chet's.

She didn't know how she'd come to like him as much as she did considering the little he'd said to her. But he had a deep-water look, an intentness that made her suspect he had interesting thoughts. If she could get him to share some of them with her, she had a hunch he'd make a good friend.

No cars were parked near the Grahams' house, but Carly heard the TV going. She knocked on the wooden part of the screen door and called, "Hellooo." When nobody answered, she stepped into the kitchen which had a faintly sour smell. Dead flies lay on the counter in front of the dusty window. Lu and Ben's spic and span kitchen was a lot more inviting.

"Hellooo," Carly called again. "Anybody home?"

"I'm in here," Gladys answered.

She was sitting in a plastic-covered recliner with a crocheted afghan draped over her shoulders. Hot as it was outside, this darkened living room was cool. Only the TV flickered colorfully. Everything else was dim.

"Hi," Carly said. "I'm sorry to bother you. I wanted to ask Chet something."

"He's gone off with his father. Some summer folk want a bid on a porch. Sit down, why don't you."

"I wanted to ask Chet about a book of mine."

"They should be back soon. Would you mind bringing me a can of soda from the fridge? I'm having one of my bad days."

Carly was glad to oblige.

"There's a bag of cookies by the bread box. See it?" Gladys called.

Carly brought the cookies too and accepted one to munch on as she sat with Gladys in the living room. A gun rack hung over the fireplace. Carly started when she saw a deer's head mounted and hung on the far wall over a couch. "Your husband hunts?" Carly asked.

"Oh, Harry's a great hunter. They always make him master of the hunt and get him to lead the drive because he knows the woods like nobody's business. I'll be glad when hunting season starts in November and Harry can forget to stew about not having no work."

Carly decided she would not, positively not, allow herself to worry about anything that far off. Instead she said, "I bet Chet has a lot of friends."

"Chet? He's got school friends, I expect. He plays ball and like that, but he'd just as soon take a fishing rod and go off alone, or with his dad, or poke around the woods."

"What does he poke around in the woods for?" Carly asked, anxiously eyeing the rack of guns.

"Well, he used to make collections of things. You know, leaves and rocks and bird nests," Gladys said. "All that stuff's probably still up there in his room. I don't bother none with the boys' rooms. Made them clean up their own mess as soon as they was old enough. It's not me's the one who spoils kids around here; it's Harry. You wouldn't believe how he worries about not having the money he promised Joe for college. 'Let the boy provide for his own education,' I told Harry. 'Let

43

him earn it and he'll appreciate it more.' But Harry says a promise is a promise."

All the while she talked, Gladys had her eyes fixed on a game show on the TV screen. Carly wondered if Gladys could really talk and attend to the game show at the same time.

An hour later Carly had wearied of hearing about Gladys's mysterious ailments and said, "I'd better be going. Would you tell Chet for me that I'll be at the deer stand this afternoon, and I'd like to ask him something?"

"Sure, I'll tell him," Gladys promised. "Close the door good when you go so the flies don't get in."

Back home, Carly had crackers and cheese and a handful of raisins. Ben, the cleanliness fanatic, had mentioned the refrigerator could use a cleaning out. Carly washed it thoroughly shelf by shelf. Then, satisfied she'd done something that would please her aunt and uncle, she took off for the deer stand with another book in hand. She read most of the afternoon, absorbed in Edith Wharton's *Ethan Frome,* a novel about thwarted love and passion in New England. Chet didn't show. She really hadn't expected he would.

*

After dinner Lu said, "Ben and I are going to a movie tonight. Want to come? It's about the Great Depression. They say it's good."

Carly looked at Ben. "You don't have to drag me along everywhere you go, you know," she said, testing for his preference in the matter.

"Hey, we're not going dancing or out with friends. It's just a movie," he said.

Carly guessed that the gesture of cleaning the refrigerator had raised her standing with him. "Well, then, sure, I'll go with you," she said. She could be lively and fun to be with, and then he'd like her even better. Anyway, she had a need for family tonight. She was feeling a little homesick.

In the car Ben mentioned that someone had sighted a bear near the Center, and Carly related an experience she and her father had had camping in Yosemite. ". . . that bear was like three feet from me and he was *huge*. My father came charging down from the privy yelling, and he ran right at that bear as if he planned to tackle it. Maybe he would have, but it turned tail and ran. I guess it thought Dad was crazy or something." Carly laughed.

"Didn't your mother ever go on your camping trips?" Lu asked.

"No. She hated bugs and sleeping on the ground. What she liked was when Dad took her to a big hotel in Acapulco or Hawaii. And she liked cities. So sometimes she went on business trips with him. Sometimes we all went and took in museums and went to concerts and things like that. Before Mother got sick, we had a lot of fun times together."

"Sounds that way," Ben said. "Pretty expensive fun."

"Well, I guess Dad makes a lot of money."

"He's in a very high-pressure business," Ben said. "It probably takes a lot out of him."

"I think he loves his work, or anyway, he says he does," Carly said. "Mother always said he had too much energy to sit still. Like you have the patience to do woodworking and build things. He doesn't."

"Everybody to their own thing," Ben said gruffly. "Your father's a big success. He deserves credit."

"Sure," Carly said, "but you lead a better life. I mean, it's healthier, and you and Lu share everything."

Ben didn't say anything to that, but later when she got intense about the depiction of human misery in the movie, he teased her in a friendly way, saying she was a character. From him, that was nearly a compliment.

She lay in bed that night thinking she was making better progress wooing Ben than Chet. How meaningful was it that he hadn't come to the deer stand? Unless Gladys had forgotten to give him the message. That was possible. Or he could just be shy of girls. After all, with all those brothers, he might not know how to talk with a girl.

She hoped it was shyness and not that he didn't like her. Most people liked her eventually. She was friendly and tried to be helpful and cooperative; so they liked her. That simple formula was something she'd learned at an early age. Of course, it might just turn out not to work on Chet. Then what? Then school, she thought. There'd be lots of kids for her next week when school began.

5

As she decided what to wear for the first day of school, Carly was remembering a line an actress friend of her father's had impressed her with once. "What you wear tells the world who you think you are." Carly thought she was easy to know but interesting. To convey that impression, she chose her favorite old cotton shirt, just nicely faded and frayed now, and her snip of a denim skirt.

The first surprise was that every girl on the school bus, and many of the boys, looked as if the price tags had just been cut off their clothes. The older girls wore bright colors, earrings, even eye makeup and heels. They weren't going to think much of her getup, Carly guessed. She looked all wrong by contrast to them.

"Hi," she said enthusiastically to the large girl on the seat beside her. The girl was friendly enough. Only she turned out to be a mature-looking sixth grader who said good-bye and got off at the elementary school, which was first among the buildings on the Consolidated School District grounds.

Next stop was the high school, an imposing brick structure with a steep roof and white-pillared portico in front. Carly thought it was handsome. Her father said buildings like that dated from a time when people showed pride in their schools by putting money into impressive architecture. Based on that theory, the seventh and eighth grade middle school, which was the last stop, had to have been built recently. It was as plain as a factory warehouse. Carly entered it chin up and expectant, though.

Remembering her own fear of new situations as a child, Lu had offered to take the morning off and accompany Carly.

"I don't need to have my hand held," Carly had assured her aunt. "I'll just find the office, introduce myself, and they'll take care of me."

"You're so independent," Lu had said with admiration. "I was Miss Shy Mouse at your age, but you— You're *really* not nervous about going alone?"

"Why should I be? School's no problem for me," Carly had said. She was a good student, better than average at sports, and popular. Those times she didn't end up as a leader, she'd been second in command or best friend to the leader. No group she'd wanted to join had ever rejected her. Now, though, she was pretending to more self-confidence than she felt as she followed the secretary's directions to 208, her homeroom.

She walked quickly through mostly empty halls past the open door of the shiny-floored gym, past the cafeteria where middle-aged ladies in hair nets were already preparing trays of food for the early lunches. The walls of the corridor were bare and so were many bulletin boards, but the glass case outside the gym was filled with basketball and track trophies.

Room 208 looked packed. A heavyset woman with short gray hair, half glasses, and orthopedic type shoes peered at the attendance card Carly handed her, then with an equal suspicion at Carly. "Well," the formidable-looking woman said, "find a seat wherever you can, but you better not be a troublemaker. I've already got more of those than I need in here."

Subdued by the negative welcome, Carly surveyed the room. Only one chair with an attached writing arm remained empty. Chet Graham had his booted feet propped on it. What luck, Carly thought and promptly claimed the chair. "Hi, Chet," she said with a smile. "I looked for you on the bus, but I didn't see you."

Some girls tittered, and the jaw of the boy behind Chet dropped open as if Carly had said something outrageous. Chet's work boots thudded to the floor. "Hi," he muttered, bending to poke through the stack of books beside his chair as if he were too busy to notice her. She'd embarrassed him again, she realized, and sank into her chair in chagrin.

Her classmates eyed her with a cool curiosity. No smiles. She was relieved when the teacher said, "All right now. Let's have your attention up here. Those of you who spent the summer hoping I'd decide to retire before school began are disappointed, I'm sure. But we made it through last year together, and I, at least, will survive this one. If you've matured any over the summer and grown some respect for learning, along with big feet—" She frowned at Chet's meaningfully. Carly turned around and saw him staring back at the teacher without expression. ". . . you may survive too. Now you know the rules. Hands up if you want to speak. Passes properly signed to leave early or come late, and *no noise*. I don't favor gum chewing any more than I did last year. I don't like troublemakers any better either." Another glance at Chet. "Any questions?"

As soon as she turned to write on the chalkboard, a spitball whizzed by Carly's head and hit the front of the teacher's desk. Carly looked over her shoulder. Chet's big hands were clasped on the arm of his chair. His face was choirboy innocent, and his long legs were stretched straight out with the soles of his boots braced against the metal legs of her chair.

She looked back at the chalkboard and read the teacher's name, Mrs. Pit. The woman was writing out their schedule. They'd have to copy it, she explained. The computer had broken down. Carly judged by the quality of silence in the classroom that Mrs. Pit was probably as tough a disciplinarian as she sounded. Never before had Carly encountered a teacher who was so openly nasty.

"She doesn't like you much, does she?" Carly whispered to Chet when the buzzer sounded for the next class.

"Not much," Chet said and hurried from the room.

Moving from class to class through the packed halls that day, Carly flashed her smile whenever anyone met her eyes. The responses were disappointing. In the minutes of freedom before classes were called to order, she used her newness as an excuse to start conversations, asking questions about ordinary things, like what the wan young English teacher's reputation was, and whether the school had after-school activities besides sports. Kids answered politely, but then turned away as if they didn't want to give her an excuse for attaching herself to them. It was eerie. Did she look so alien to them in her faded shirt?

"Hey," she wanted to yell in the cafeteria where she'd smiled her way into a table with three boys sitting at one end and two girls at the other, "I showered and washed my hair, and I'm a nice person."

The kids at the table had said sure, she could sit there, but then they had ignored her. Their conversation had something to do with the county fair and prizes one of the girls had won for her goats. Carly had listened politely, waiting for an opportunity to make a remark.

"Did you hear about Dwayne's brother?"

"My dad said it served him right. He's always showing off."

"Yeah, but it's too bad, I mean, losing an eye—"

"He could've wound up dead."

"How'd he get hurt?" Carly asked, but no one seemed to hear her.

Lunch hour passed and she still hadn't struck up an acquaintance with anyone. Lunchtime was always the best opportunity to meet people, and somehow she'd muffed it. She was so rattled that she raised her hand when Mrs. Pit, who turned out to be their social studies teacher, announced they were starting off with a unit on the organization of the federal government and asked if anyone knew what the branches of government were. "Executive, legislative and judicial," Carly answered, "or the president, Congress and the Supreme Court."

"Your school do that unit last year?" Mrs. Pit asked.

"No," Carly said. "But I read the newspaper."

"Do you indeed," Mrs. Pit said. "Then you can be in charge of keeping the current events bulletin board up-to-date. All right?"

"Sure," Carly agreed.

Someone snickered as if Carly had just been tricked. Weird, she thought. This whole school was weird.

She approached Mrs. Pit after class to ask if someone could work with her on the bulletin board project.

"You find someone who wants to do it with you, it's fine with me," Mrs. Pit said. "Do a good job, and you'll get extra credit towards your first quarter's grade."

"Could you ask someone for me, please?" Carly said politely. "I'm new, after all, and I wouldn't know who—"

"Wouldn't do you any good for me to assign anyone. These kids don't do work they're not absolutely responsible for. They don't read newspapers anyway. Whatever news they get comes from the TV." She narrowed her eyes. "But believe you me, I'll see to it they learn how this country operates before I'm finished with them. Well, if you don't want to do it . . ."

Carly considered. The task might offer opportunities. "I'm willing to try," she said, "as long as I can stop if nobody shows any interest."

"All right." Mrs. Pit looked at Carly more kindly. She even smiled. The smile didn't cheer Carly any. Winning the approval of teachers was a given for her. This unfriendly student body was the real challenge.

As she walked along the line of waiting buses after school, Carly saw a motorcycle go by with two boys on it. The tall one behind the driver was Chet. So that was why she hadn't seen him on the bus. She hoped he didn't get a ride on the motorcycle every day.

Since no one sat beside her on the way home, she set herself to considering the current events bulletin board. She might get kids talking to her if she could interest them in what she put up—humor, of course, cartoons, and human interest stories. There had to be a local newspaper full of items with names familiar to her classmates. Lu and Ben might have some good ideas too. Ben came from a rural area like this one in Massachusetts, and although Lu had been brought up in Los

53

Angeles, she'd probably sized up the local population in the five years she'd lived here, especially since she worked with kids who visited the Environmental Education Center on field trips.

With that decided, Carly started thinking about Chet Graham. He didn't appear to be a gifted and talented type, that was sure. "Troublemaker," Mrs. Pit had said and looked at Chet meaningfully. Then the spitball. Judging by direction, it must have come from him. He'd been daring as well as childish, considering Mrs. Pit. Was he as interesting as she had guessed he might be when she'd met him in the woods? Or was he just one of those kids who hated school and preferred not to work his brain too hard? If he hated Mrs. Pit, it was understandable. Sour as that lady was, she *should* have retired.

Carly wished she had made a friend she could talk things over with, even if it was only by phone.

She'd spent too much time alone lately, more than she'd ever spent except for the week after her mother's funeral. That week Carly had refused to go back to day camp although her father had returned to work and didn't like leaving her home alone. Stubbornly, she'd insisted. She'd felt she owed it to her mother to mourn her, but actually, Carly hadn't felt much. To bring on the tears, she'd deliberately gone over all the photograph albums in the house and then started packing up her mother's things. Still, the numbness remained.

Her father had been shocked when he discovered her loading boxes with the contents of her mother's closet. "What are you doing that for?" he'd demanded.

"Someone has to do it."

"The cleaning woman can take care of it. Don't be morbid, Carly. She's at rest now, and it's time you relaxed and had some fun again."

"I can't," she'd said. "I feel too guilty."

"Why? You did the best you could."

"No," she'd said. If he hadn't turned away from her then, she would have tried to explain to him what she regretted, like being so favored by him that even in the good times when they had all three been together, Mother was always the odd man out. Carly cringed to recall how she'd reveled in her father's preference for her. Mother had been the better person. All Mother had cared about was making them happy while Carly and her father only cared about themselves.

"You didn't love her very much, Dad," Carly had accused him over the top of the magazine he'd picked up to shut her out.

Without looking up, he'd said defensively, "I loved her. Not as much as she wanted me to maybe. . . . We had an okay marriage, as good as most people I know."

"And you think *you* did the best you could for her while she was sick?"

He'd flinched. Then he'd looked at her and said earnestly, "Listen, life's too short to waste any part of it in unnecessary suffering. I did what I could. Your mother

seemed satisfied. She understood my limits just the way
I understood hers."

"Well, *I* don't understand," Carly had yelled.

"Who says you have to?" he'd yelled back. "It's not
up to you to pass judgment on your mother's and my
relationship."

Why couldn't he just admit that he'd failed Mother
and be sorry about it? It galled Carly that he felt he'd
done no wrong. It galled her most to find out he wasn't
wonderful after all.

*

The A-frame was too empty for Carly after that first
day of school and she escaped to the deer stand. The
day's disappointments continued there. The clearing was
empty of deer. She wished she'd brought a notepad and
pen along to write a message to Chet. "I'm here. Wish
you were because I need to ask you something." What
she wanted to ask him was what was making everyone
back off from her. Probably he wouldn't be able to
answer anyway. She wondered if he had taken the Tolkien
book. He could be reading it now. If he had enough
imagination to enjoy fantasy, they might become friends
yet.

Wearily, she climbed out of the tree and headed back
to the house by a different route. A movement in the
bushes caught her eye. She froze while her eyes picked
out a leg from the similar shapes of brown stems—a leg
and a bobbing head. The doe. It was a minute before
Carly realized it was one of her fawns that the doe was

licking. The tenderness of it thrilled Carly and suddenly her eyes were full. For a long while she stood crying silently for her mother, for herself, and for all the lovingness that she'd never appreciated until it was gone.

The doe with her fawn had been a sign, Carly told herself when she finally continued on her way. She'd make friends here. Of course she would. Somebody was bound to like her, somebody she could like back. She just had to keep trying.

6

That whole first week of school whenever Lu asked how her day had gone, Carly answered, "Fine," and changed the subject. But Friday after dinner she broke down and told the truth. "It isn't working, Lu. Mrs. Pit's my only friend, and you can imagine how popular *that* makes me with the other kids." She dried some of the silverware and put it away in the drawer. "Any ideas on what I could be doing wrong?"

Lu looked sympathetic as she scrubbed a pot and considered the question. "I can't imagine," she said, "unless you're just being friendly to the wrong people."

"What do you mean?"

"Well, there have to be some shy, quiet kids who don't have any friends and who'd be glad to be noticed by someone as lively as you."

Ben rattled his newspaper, and when they glanced across the counter at him, he offered his opinion. "You've only been there a week, Carly. Most of those kids have known each other all their lives."

Lu nodded as she set the pot to drain in the wooden rack. "Ben's probably right. You just have to be patient."

"I think it's more than that," Carly said. "They look at me out of the corner of their eyes like they just don't *like* me. I'm not used to being looked at that way." Her lip betrayed her by quivering.

"Oh, honey, you must be imagining things," Lu said in a buttery voice that melted the last of Carly's pride.

"It's true," Carly said. "Something's wrong with me."

In the living room Ben's paper rattled purposefully again. "I can tell you what's wrong, but you won't like it," he said.

"Then be quiet," Lu told him. "Can't you see how bad she feels? Don't you remember how important friends were when you were her age?"

"Friends are important at any age. I married you so I'd have a permanent friend, didn't I?" Ben asked.

Lu beamed at him. She dried her wet hands and walked around the counter to plop herself down on her husband's lap. "Sometimes you say the nicest things," she murmured and kissed him.

"I do?" he asked. He grinned. "Then why don't you trust me to tell Carly anything?"

"*I* trust you," Carly said. "Let's hear it."

"Okay. You're a city girl in a country school. You talk too fast and know too much, and I bet they're not comfortable with you."

"Ben!" Lu cried. "That's mean."

He shrugged. "What do you say, Carly? Think I'm being mean?"

Carly shook her head. "No. But if you're right, what can I do about it?" The situation seemed hopeless because, while she could change her behavior, she couldn't change who she was.

"I expect they'll accept you eventually," Ben said. "Meanwhile, you can try toning yourself down a little."

"Maybe you could go out for soccer or volleyball," Lu said. "Or join a 4-H club. That'd be good."

Carly shook her head. "I'm not *that* desperate."

"Now there," Ben moved Lu off his lap so he could stand up and expound. "That's the kind of nose-in-the-air attitude that puts these kids off. What's wrong with volleyball or a 4-H club?"

"Nothing," Carly said. "You're right, Ben. Thanks."

He was right, but she wasn't about to raise her own calves or goats or sew her own clothes or bump a ball over a net when those activities didn't interest her. There *were* girls in her class with interests she shared. Sarah and Jane for instance. Sarah was a talented artist and Jane had a quick wit. They were inseparable and both liked boys. It was their table that Carly had tried to join the first day of school and again a couple of days later. She knew better now, and ate her sandwich in the art room where she was inconspicuous and could pass the time trying to learn how to draw deer from a book.

Kim was another girl who attracted Carly. Kim was very tall and quiet, a natural athlete who shone in gym class where everybody cheered as she led the pack running the six hundred. She had broken the high jump and hurdle records in seventh grade, but what interested Carly most was that Kim had just lost her father. Carly had tried talking to her about their common experience once when they happened to be alone in the girls' room, standing at adjoining sinks. "Were you very close to your father?" Carly had asked.

Kim had look startled. "What?"

"I heard you lost your father, and I was wondering. My mother died this summer."

"I d-don't like to talk about it," Kim had stuttered. Afterward she looked the other way whenever she couldn't avoid being near Carly.

As for Chet Graham, even though he sat right behind her in homeroom, he maintained a quiet zone between them. She thought maybe she'd insulted him by asking if he knew what had happened to the book she'd left on the deer stand. "I didn't take it," he'd answered quickly, and hadn't listened to her assurance that she hadn't meant to accuse him of anything. Besides, he concentrated all his energies in school on making mischief without getting caught and was always on the list of people who hadn't handed in their assignments.

"That Chet Graham," Mrs. Pit had complained to Carly one lunch hour when they were alone together in the homeroom while Mrs. Pit marked papers and Carly tacked articles up on the bulletin board. "It's disgraceful that he hands in a careless paper like this when he's got more brains than his brother Joe ever had. Joe was a straight A student, but Chet just doesn't care."

It intrigued Carly to watch Chet appear well behaved and polite all the while he was sailing paper airplanes through the classroom, or opening windows so that five minutes of the period had to be spent retrieving the test papers that had been piled on the teacher's desk. He tormented Mrs. Pit, behaved himself for the hard-of-hearing math teacher, and was indulged by the wan young English teacher, who tried valiantly to lead them through the battlefield of a grammar review. The grammar was boring to Carly, and like the rest of the class, she was amused when tremors in the room turned out not to be the earthquake Ms. Hauser imagined but Chet bouncing his heavy heels against the floor.

The most avid reader in the class was Melvin, a loner who'd cringed as if she was attacking him when Carly saw him reading *Lord of the Flies* under his desk and asked how he was enjoying it. Carly cringed too at the possibility of having to spend her time in school as an outsider indefinitely. She didn't think she could stand it. On the other hand, she wasn't ready to give up and go home to her father. While she'd be happier in her old school, her father would take her return as de facto forgiveness and she wasn't letting him off the hook that easily.

Carly had just tucked herself around her pillow and closed her eyes Friday evening when Ben called her downstairs for a phone call.

"Who is it?" she asked, not budging because she knew who it was. Eleven o'clock was too late for local people to be calling, but it was only eight in L.A.

"Come on down and find out," Ben said.

"No. Just tell him I'm doing fine," she said and clenched her pillow.

She heard Ben speaking angrily to Lu after he'd hung up. No doubt he was talking about Carly's attitude toward her father again. Ben would never approve of her so long as he identified so strongly with her father. But Ben wasn't *like* her father. If Lu were dying, Ben wouldn't retreat and keep retreating. Ben was no coward. Probably he'd be more tender and loving than ever, and that was how it should be, the way it should have been for Mother.

Of course, Ben had other reasons for not being too crazy about his niece by marriage. He and Lu wouldn't have picked an isolated place like this to live in if they hadn't valued their privacy, and Carly knew she was intruding on it. She had heard them through the wall of their bedroom at night murmuring and shushing each other when they got too loud. She wished she had somewhere else to go, someplace where someone would hug her once in a while as Lu did.

"Mother," she whispered into the pillow. "Oh, Mama, I'm sorry." Her own coldness haunted Carly—that afternoon before they knew Mother was sick when Carly had been reading a book of poetry and Mother had coaxed, "Come sit on my lap, and we'll read together."

"I'm too old to sit on your lap, Mother. Stop treating me like a baby."

"You still sit on your father's lap."

"That's different. Can't you see I'm as tall as you are now?" She'd ignored the tears in Mother's eyes. Mother had always cried too easily, been hurt too easily, even before the cancer. Like her father, Carly admired strong, buoyant people. Now she lay in bed in a house where she didn't really belong and wondered if her efforts to be loving to her Mother at the end could possibly have made up for what she hadn't given Mother before.

"Want to read William Blake to me, Ma?" Carly had asked the wax figure lying so sadly still in the hospital bed.

"Not now, darling. I'm too tired."

"Want *me* to read to you?"

"Yes, that would be lovely. Thank you."

" 'Little lamb, who made thee? Was it God who made thee?' . . . "

With Mother's eyes on her, still full of love.

Mother had forgiven her. Of course Mother, being soft and gentle, had forgiven her. But she and her father

64

had hurt Mother's feelings so often, behaving as if her hunger for love and her lovingness was something to be scorned. Carly wished it hadn't taken cancer to make her kind. She wished so hard that the purple pain came rushing back. She clutched the pillow and gritted her teeth and still she couldn't bear it.

*

Monday, during homeroom, Carly took down the local news and sports articles. A few students had glanced at them, but no one had commented on them to her. Mrs. Pit hadn't been too pleased with Carly's selection either. "Were *those* your idea of the most important news stories of the week, Carly?"

Still bent on capturing students' interest rather than teacher's approval, Carly tacked up newspaper photographs highlighted by black arrows and handwritten headlines about the forest fire raging only twenty miles away. She used the reddest construction paper she could find as background.

Chet stood in front of the board and read the whole thing. One of Sarah and Jane's boyfriends joined him saying, "My uncle's over there fighting that one." Chet grunted.

Carly was tacking up the last article. "Does your uncle expect the fire to do much damage?" she asked the boy.

"It's already took half the mountain."

"How awful," Carly said.

"The lake will stop it before it gets anybody's house," Chet said.

"But what about the animals?" Carly asked.

Chet and the boy looked at her as if she were simpleminded. "Some get out and some don't," the boy said.

She thought of her deer and suddenly the fire was real to her. But the deer would escape. They couldn't be trapped by fire. Snakes and frogs and turtles maybe, but nothing beautiful that could run or fly. "Chet," she said, "the deer wouldn't die in a forest fire, would they?"

"Might," he said. "Sometimes they panic and go the wrong way." He slid into his seat as she shivered.

If her deer family were ever in danger, she would run to the woods and get them out somehow. She'd never let them die, she vowed to herself.

After school she went to the deer stand as usual. She thought they knew her now, recognized her. They didn't run even when she made a twig snap by mistake and their ears came up, heads alert, ready. "It's just that girl who watches us," she imagined them thinking. She pretended that they understood that they were hers, her beautiful family who needed her to care for them.

In the stillness she saw a leaf twirl slowly to the ground, not from the white oak but from a tree whose leaves had all turned yellow within the past week. The woods were tarnished now with shades of brass and rust.

"Nothing's more beautiful than this country when the leaves turn in the fall," Ben had said.

Except my deer, Carly thought. She wished she had Sarah's ability to draw. Her own attempts to sketch the

66

deer had been so bad, she'd torn them up. What she needed was her camera. Her father would mail it if she asked him, but she wasn't about to ask him for favors.

She borrowed Ben's camera on Tuesday, but no deer appeared. Besides, she could tell by Ben's fussiness as he showed her how to use the camera and cautioned her about carrying it in the woods that he'd been reluctant to lend it to her. "It's a good one," he'd told her, meaning, "Be careful; it's expensive."

The next morning at breakfast Ben asked her if she'd finished using the camera yet, and she handed it back to him without a word, unused. His only reaction was a look of relief.

"I'm doing okay," she reassured herself later that week as she scrambled up the elephant-hide rock and threaded her way through the green-and-gold woods to the deer stand. She had the deer and Lu, and she'd make out fine. Whatever happened, she'd endure.

It was then she heard the gunshot. It came from the direction of the gully, or maybe even beyond that. She rushed to the gully, her blood pulsing in her ears as she imagined her deer under attack. The gully was empty of everything but brambles and the ribbon of wetness at the bottom. Another shot. She started out again toward the Grahams' old orchard. It didn't occur to her that what she was doing was dangerous. Protecting her deer family was her only thought.

The boy was much shorter than Chet.

"What are you shooting at?" she yelled at him.

He swung around to look at her with the muzzle pointed at the sky.

"None of your business," he said. Then he glared at her from a tight, strong-featured face that was a crude version of Chet's and added, "You're trespassing on Graham property."

"It's not hunting season yet."

He grinned evilly. "You the new game warden?"

"Are you Joe?"

"Go on home," he said, "you're bothering me."

She didn't like the way he was looking at her. She didn't like the look of him at all. With deliberate slowness she turned around and walked back through the woods. He wasn't likely to shoot anything, knowing she'd seen him and might tell the game warden.

Saturday morning Carly jumped to her feet and ran out of the house, wild with excitement when she caught sight of Chet coming up the driveway. She was sure he'd relented and was going to be sociable after all.

"Hi," she greeted him joyously. "How are you?"

He stopped short and stared at her in alarm. "Fine," he said.

"Didn't you come over to see me?" she asked more calmly.

"Yeah. I found your book." He took the paperback copy of Tolkien out of his pocket. It looked more tattered and limp than she remembered. "My brother had it."

"Your brother?" She hoped the book wasn't his only reason for coming.

"Joe. He found it on the deer stand and was reading it."

"Did he like it?"

"He didn't say. . . . I guess he must've or he wouldn't of read it."

"You ever read Tolkien?"

"No," Chet said.

"Keep it then. You might enjoy him."

"I'm not much for reading." He thrust the book at her.

"You mean except for westerns." She had seen him devouring paperbacks under his desk during classes when he wasn't staring out the window or shooting spitballs.

"Yeah, I like those pretty well."

"I met your brother in the apple orchard. He was shooting at something. He wouldn't tell me what."

"Just target practice probably." Chet turned to go.

Disappointment broke her down. "Chet," she said. "Tell me something please?"

"What?"

"What is it about me that nobody here likes?"

"Nothing. You're okay." His blue eyes searched her face.

"Please," she begged. "Just give me a clue. I must be doing something wrong or—Nobody sits with me at lunch. Nobody talks to me. It's like I'm diseased or something."

"You go after them too hard," he said in the deep man's rumble that came on him at times.

"Thanks," she said. He had offered something, not enough, but at least he had answered her as if she existed for him. She opened her mouth and closed it. If she pushed further, he'd retreat. Like the deer, she thought.

"See you Monday," she said before his long legs took him away from her.

She thought it funny that, with all his unmatched big muscular and thin parts, Chet should move so gracefully. And they'd had a real conversation! She'd begun to think she'd never experience the coziness of talking out her heart to anyone here but Lu.

What would it take to make Chet into a friend? He was as elusive as the deer, but even they were getting used to her. Maybe he would too, in time, if she could make herself be patient and just watch and wait.

7

That morning Carly wasn't looking for her deer. She was collecting varieties of fall leaves for an exhibit Ben was preparing for the Center. He'd been pleased by her offer of help and eagerly taught her to identify ash and butternut and shagbark hickory trees by their leaves and bark. He was a man who loved teaching, Carly decided.

She was making notes on striation, color, and texture differences between the bark of two trees with similar lemony leaves when something moved in a nearby clump of bushes. Instinctively, she flattened herself against the nearest tree trunk.

The buck looked like hers. He had his head down and seemed to be trying to saw through the tangle of branches with his antlers. When he pulled free and brought his head up, Carly was horrified. Bloody, torn and tattered matter hung from his horns. Again, he bowed his head and resumed the agonized rubbing against the branches. She didn't know what was wrong with him. All she knew was that she had to rescue him from his misery somehow.

Ben and Lu would know what to do. She could call them, but the Center was so far away. They'd never make it home in less than half an hour even if they could leave immediately. The buck might be dead by then.

Chet was closer. Instantly, Carly dropped her bag of leaves and her notebook and raced off, zigzagging through trees and around bramble patches toward the Grahams' house.

She heard a chain saw screaming before the house came in sight, and she veered off into the woods in the direction of the noise. Sure enough, there were both Chet and his father. Harry Graham was cutting through the trunk of a fair-sized tree, and Chet was whacking an ax against branches lying on the ground. Small stove-sized logs were piled near him.

Mr. Graham quieted his chain saw to yell at her, "Stay where you are till I get this tree down. Don't move now."

A minute later, the trunk crashed to the ground, and he pushed his hard hat up from his forehead and said, "Okay, come ahead now." He pulled a cord and his machine started whining again.

"Chet!" Carly stood close to him so he could hear her. "Something terrible's happened. My buck's all bloody."

Chet halted with his ax in the air and looked at her with concern in his vivid blue eyes. "Somebody shot him?"

"I don't know, but he's over by the deer stand acting weird."

Chet set his ax aside and yelled to get his father's attention. Harry stopped sawing the trunk into manageable lengths long enough to ask, "What's up?" The sudden absence of noise was a relief.

"The buck's horns are all bloody and torn," Carly explained. "He looks terrible, and I'm afraid—"

"Blood on his horns?" Harry asked. He grinned. "Got kind of raggedy stuff hanging from them too?"

"Oh," Chet said. "That's what it is."

"That's what what is?" Carly demanded. "What can we do to save him?"

Harry's belly laugh made Carly furious. "What are you laughing about? He's hurt. Just because he's an animal doesn't mean he can't suffer."

"You tell her, Chet. She had you going good there for a minute, didn't she?" Harry gave a last chuckle, then took a drink from a plastic milk container filled with water.

Carly would have liked to sock him. "I don't see what's so funny," she said to Chet.

"The buck's okay," Chet said. "They always rub the velvet off their antlers in the fall, and the velvet's like skin with blood vessels in it. So before they get their horns clean, it can look pretty messy."

"I guess you didn't know that," Harry said in a kindly way, but his smile didn't cool Carly's indignation.

"When you said he was bloody, I thought maybe a poacher got him," Chet said. "I was just about ready to get my rifle and finish him off."

"Kill my buck?" Now she was appalled at Chet.

"Well, you don't want to leave a wounded deer to suffer. You've got to put it out of its misery," Chet explained.

"That's brutal. That's savage," Carly said.

"Oh, now, don't you be so quick to pass judgment," Harry said. "We take our deer hunting seriously around here, and we respect the whitetail, like the Indians used to, even though we go after deer with guns instead of bows and arrows mostly."

"Do *you* hunt them?" Carly asked Chet. It horrified her to think she'd misinterpreted his interest in her deer.

Chet shrugged but Harry said gleefully, "I could tell you a story about what kind of hunter Chet here is."

"Come on, Pop!" Chet begged. "Not that one again."

"But she never heard it," Harry said. He eased himself down on the raw blond wood of a newly made stump to tell his tale. "One mean November morning a couple of years back, I shook Chet awake before dawn. See, he'd been badgering me to take him hunting with me. 'Get up,' I said and told him where I was taking up a stand near a certain deer runway. Told him to follow me shortly and drive the deer toward where I'd be waiting with the gun."

Harry stopped to rub his nose and shove his glasses into place. "Well, it was cold out there standing up against a tree and trying hard not to scratch my head or let the rising sun glint on my glasses so's the deer'd spot me. But I waited a good long while, and suddenly out of the mist steps this beauty of a pronghorn. Well, before you know it, I had that buck shot and was dressing him out, never doubting that Chet had driven him to me like he was supposed to. Naturally, I expected Chet to show up any second to see what we got, but he never showed. Finally, I'm lugging the carcass home by myself and along comes Chet, apologizing all over the place. Seems he'd fallen back to sleep and never done his part at all."

Harry laughed, then waited for Carly's response to what he obviously considered a very funny story. When she remained silent, he carefully explained the joke to her. "Now as to how that deer got there, well, he must have just happened along by accident, see?"

She stared at him, this ghoulish man who had seemed so genial the first time she'd met him. Then she turned to Chet. How could a boy with a face as angelic as his be a killer?

"I guess where you come from they don't do much deer hunting," Harry finally concluded. "Don't know much about it?"

"Nothing," she said. She didn't want to know anything either. The very idea made her feel like taking the next plane back to Los Angeles, but she wouldn't desert her deer, not when hunting season was only a few weeks off and she was their only ally.

"Why'nt you come to the house for some lunch," Harry suggested, "and I'll educate you on the whitetail deer. It's my favorite subject."

She accepted the invitation, not for the pleasure of their company, but in the grim need to know the enemy.

Lunch was tuna fish salad, a very tasty tuna fish salad surrounded by tomatoes and accompanied by pickles and a pot of coffee and slabs of thick white bread that appeared to be home-baked. "Gladys makes the best tuna fish salad in the county," Harry announced as he served himself a generous helping.

"The bread is delicious too," Carly said. She was surprised to find Gladys capable of doing anything, having imagined her invalided permanently in her chair.

"Harry baked the bread," Gladys said.

"It's my therapy," Harry said. "Nights I can't fall asleep, I go to the kitchen and put up some dough. Nothing like kneading that nice soft dough to soothe a man. Also the smell of it baking makes me delirious."

"Delirious is what you are all right," Gladys teased. "Beats me what a character like you's doing with a good straightforward son like Chet."

Carly looked wide-eyed at Chet who smiled down at his plate. Apparently his parents had no idea of how he behaved in school.

"Never mind, Gladys. My character's not what interests this little girl here. I'm gonna educate her on the whitetail deer," Harry said.

"Harry loves the deer," Gladys said to Carly. "He lives for deer hunting season. Don't matter what the weather's like; come deer hunting season, Harry's out there in it."

Carly stiffened.

"Eat," Gladys said, and Carly ate as Harry began to ramble on about how, in bygone times, deer were so important that men used to be paid in buckskins or "bucks."

" . . . When I was a boy, just starting out, they cut off my shirt tail for missing a shot on a drive with the men. Made me take my target practice serious, let me tell you. First thing a hunter should be is a good shot."

Harry took a big bite of bread before he continued. "Then he's got to know his deer. Now the deer, they'll stand in a field in the summertime eating your crops and watching you clearing out the weeds, and so long as you don't make a move toward them, they're bold as brass. But comes the first day of hunting season and those very same deer disappear. They got a sixth sense of when they're in danger."

"But they get killed," Carly said.

"Well, a man's got more brains than a deer, after all. So some deer get killed, but they're good breeders. There are more deer alive in this country today than when the

Indians hunted them. See, the deer can't find enough to eat in a real forest, but second-growth places have lots of tender green shoots and twigs low enough for them to reach up and nip. And they like what a farmer grows too—alfalfa and clover and corn and celery and cabbage. In some ways they're like cows, even to having several stomachs. Except deer are nervous animals. Anything will spook them."

By the time lunch was over, the very ease and volume of Harry's talking had dissipated some of Carly's anger.

"You and Chet care to do the dishes while Gladys and I rest from our labors?" Harry asked, and Carly found herself with a dish towel in her hands, feeling oddly as if Harry had tamed her as she dried the dishes Chet handed her.

"He didn't mean anything by laughing at you back there in the woods," Chet said.

"That wasn't what made me so angry," she answered, glad that Chet had been sensitive enough to recognize her anger. "It's the deer. I'll die if those deer get killed, Chet. They're mine."

"Wild animals don't belong to anybody."

"These do."

"Come deer season, they'll probably disappear out of their regular places, just like my father said. They can take care of themselves."

"I want you to help me protect them."

"Me? I'm planning on going deer hunting myself."

She slapped the towel against the counter. "You'd shoot those fawns?"

"No, and not the doe either, but the buck's fair game. Though next year would be better when he's bigger."

"You're a monster," she said and backed away from him. "You don't have any feelings at all."

Without waiting to tender a polite thank-you for the lunch, she dashed out of the house and ran home. She arrived panting and miserable.

It was only after she had bathed herself and simmered down that she remembered she'd left the collection of leaves in the woods where she'd seen the buck scraping the velvet off his antlers. Wearily, she made her way back to the spot and picked up the bag of leaves and the notebook.

No deer to be seen. How was she going to protect them? Suppose she lured them into Lu and Ben's back-yard and kept them so well fed that they stayed put there? Then she could get Ben to post his land so that nobody could hunt on it without his permission. She could probably work on Chet too. He might be a hunter, but he couldn't really be as heartless as she had accused him of being. Yes, she'd try to tame the deer and get Ben to help her, and she'd also try to reach Chet.

Just having a plan of action cheered her. She selected a book of short stories from Lu and Ben's haphazard library and sat down to read.

8

In Los Angeles, Carly had always been able to talk out her emotional storms with her mother or father or friends. Here she had only Lu and Ben. She was so impatient for them to get home that she couldn't settle into the book she was reading. She jittered about, then began to discharge some of her nervous energy by assembling an enormous cold salad of leftover vegetables, tomatoes and lettuce.

Harry Graham's home-baked bread would have complemented the salad well, Carly thought, and wondered how it was possible that a man who liked to bake bread could be a killer. Fangs would suit him better than that amiable smile. Not that his smile would ever deceive her again. He wanted to kill her deer; therefore he was the enemy.

Supper was ready and her aunt and uncle still weren't home. Carly set the table, then got some chrysanthemums and spruce branches from the yard to make a centerpiece for it.

Ben looked amazed when he walked into the kitchen. "Well, well, well, what's the occasion, Carly?"

"I just felt like doing something," she said.

"This was at the post office," Lu said, handing Carly a letter from her father. "Thanks for making the dinner. I'm pooped tonight."

"Not too pooped to talk to me, I hope," Carly said. I've got a problem." She opened the envelope and scanned the one page with her father's bold handwriting. His letters were usually businesslike reports on his status without anecdotes or expressions of feeling, but this one was different.

Dear Carly,
I'm working evenings and most weekends trying to close on a deal that'd set me up for life. Even though I'm busy, I miss you, but considering how little I'm home, it may be just as well that you're not hanging around waiting for me. Although, if you'd been here, you could've gone with me up to San Francisco this week and had some sourdough bread and a cable car ride. I remember how nutty you were about the cable car the first time you saw it. You must've been about six. How about sending me a letter? Or pick up the phone if you don't want to write, and tell me when we're getting together. I miss you, kid.
Your loving father.

For him, that was an emotional letter. He'd enclosed her usual generous weekly allowance check. Carly handed it over to Lu to bank for her along with the part of the weekly expense money Dad sent that Lu judged was excessive. Carly could have told her father there was nothing for her to buy in this town. Even the shopping mall Lu and Ben sometimes trekked an hour to get to didn't offer much of interest. But having money could come in handy sometime; so Carly kept accepting the checks. She knew money meant little to her father. What he valued was his own time and energy, and those she would continue to refuse.

Lu served the salad accompanied by glasses of milk and last night's corn bread. It was dry because Ben had overbaked it. "So what's the problem?" Lu asked as they took their usual places around the table.

"I had the most awful experience this afternoon," Carly began. While Lu and Ben ate, she described her horror at seeing the buck with the bloody shreds hanging from his horns and how she'd run to the Grahams for help and how Mr. Graham had laughed at her.

"And then, and *then*, I find out he and Chet are planning to shoot my buck. Can you believe it? They've got the deer stand up in the tree, *not* because they love animals so much, but to keep track of the deer so they can find them and *kill* them." She stopped because her voice had gone shrill.

"Isn't it possible your friend Chet does enjoy watching the deer?" Ben suggested.

Carly thought about it, remembering how Chet had pointed out the deer to her the first time she'd seen them. "So what if he does?" she said. "That just makes it worse."

"Hunting's the favorite sport around here, Carly," Lu said, carefully explaining the obvious. "Some pretty nice people hunt."

"You don't think it's rotten to get acquainted with innocent animals just so you can murder them more easily? You don't think that's hateful, Lu?"

"Put that way," Lu said, "it does sound bad."

"Harry Graham's got a reputation as a very ethical hunter," Ben said. "They say he'll forego his own hunting to track deer other hunters have wounded. He's hiked deep into the back country just to dispatch them in a humane way."

"Killing deer can't be humane," Carly protested.

"Come on, Carly, I'm not a hunter myself, but the fact is, Harry's a good sportsman."

"I'm with you, Carly," Lu said. "I think it's disgusting that all those armed men run around shooting up the woods and making it dangerous to leave your own house. But I don't like football or prizefights or bullfighting either. They're all brutal, bloody male sports."

"Male sports!" Ben objected. "Let's not forget the Amazons and Diana, the huntress."

"Diana was a myth," Lu said. "Sure there are female hunters, but basically, it's a male activity."

Carly brought them back to the problem at hand. "Just tell me how I can save my buck."

"You can't," Ben said flatly.

"Why can't I? I could lure him onto your property, and if you posted your land so no one could hunt on it—"

"What are you going to lure him with? Food? He'll eat and run. Deer are pretty territorial," Ben told her. "They spend their lives within an area of a square mile or so. Your buck probably already crisscrosses our land, and even if you set up a salt lick or something to tempt him, he's going to go back into the Grahams' woods when he feels like it."

"What's a salt lick?" Carly asked.

"Basically a solid block of salt. Cows like licking it and so do deer."

"Maybe if we made a fenced-in area and trapped him inside—just during hunting season," Carly suggested.

"Honey, deer can soar right over an eight-foot fence from a standing start," Ben said. "A deer's shoulders are only connected to its body by muscle tissue. They're very resilient animals. They can bound twenty feet in a single leap and crawl through a ditch on their bellies to sneak past a hunter. They'll even circle around behind a hunter, and they can swim well too. They're anything but easy game. Your buck's not helpless."

Carly set her mouth stubbornly against the flood of information. "But the Grahams are stalking him already," she said. "They're studying his habits. He's practically in their gunsights."

"Actually," Lu said, "the deer *must* be outwitting the hunters around here, because they're increasing according to government census."

"Right," Ben said. "The population only shrinks when they starve to death after a really bad winter. If nobody hunted, Carly, the deer would outstrip the local food supply. Would you rather see them weeded out by starvation?"

"Then you *do* approve of hunting?" Carly asked.

Ben shrugged. "I'm just giving you the facts. And the fact is nature's cruel too."

"The fact is, hunting a beautiful healthy animal is vicious," Carly said.

Ben threw his hands up. "I surrender. You want the land posted. Okay, we'll post it."

"Good," Carly said. "What should I feed them?"

"You going to pay for it?" he asked.

"Of course. I've got lots of money and I can't think of a better way to spend it."

Ben suggested a salt lick and apples to start with. "We can buy windfalls," he said. "The Cider Mill's on our way home from work. But you don't want to make those deer come too close to the house. The clearing where we tore down the old barn might be the best place." He got a flashlight to take Carly out back and show her where he meant.

Lu winked at Carly and said, "Looks like you've hooked him good."

The first few nights the half bushel of apples Carly scattered around disappeared all right, but Ben judged by the tracks in the soft ground that raccoons, not deer, had taken the apples. The No Hunting signs he'd ordered were printed, and Carly nailed them onto trees along the property lines Ben pointed out to her. By that time, the deer had joined the raccoons, and the apple consumption was up to half a wheelbarrow a night. The salt lick was doing a good business too.

One evening after dinner, Carly enveloped herself in Ben's down-filled winter jacket and crouched on the hood of Lu and Ben's car where she could watch for the deer without disturbing them. Her nose was chilled, but otherwise the oversized jacket protected her from the frosty late October air. An amazing pumpkin-colored moon, bigger and fatter than any she had ever seen, hung in the sky above the treetops. She was so fascinated by it that she missed seeing the deer arrive, but suddenly they were there. She couldn't be positive in the dark, but she thought she saw her buck among them. At least one head crowned with antlers was etched with a special grace against the inky sky.

That night she woke up screaming. She didn't know why. Only a trace of fear remained and a sense of darkness. Ben stuck his head around the partition between their rooms and asked, "You all right?"

"I'm okay. Just a bad dream."

He yawned widely and stumbled over to kiss the top of her head as if she were a little girl. "Go to sleep then," he said and returned to his bedroom.

It comforted Carly to realize Ben was getting fond of her after all. Also, the bouts of purple pain weren't coming as often or lasting as long, and as for the deer, she thought they were spending more time on Lu and Ben's property than the Grahams' now. She touched the letter she kept under her pillow, the one in which her father had written that he missed her. He hadn't called in a while. It figured that *he* wouldn't suffer long. Hadn't he said life was too short to waste it suffering? She didn't let herself think about missing him. She squeezed her eyes shut against thinking and struggled to get to sleep.

School remained a disappointment. Every conversation Carly started fizzled out. She hadn't made any real friends and still retreated to the art teacher's room during lunchtime. Since her skill at copying pictures of deer hadn't shown any improvement, all she did there now was read.

The brave Ms. Hauser handed back their tests on the grammar unit and told them, "Now we can do a unit that's really fun—poetry."

Half the class groaned, but Ms. Hauser maintained her smile. "You'll see," she told them confidently. "You're going to enjoy this."

It looked like disaster in the making to Carly. She could not imagine these impassive eighth graders responding positively to anything lyrical or emotional. They'd be bored or worse, mocking. Ms. Hauser would be crushed and Carly, who couldn't keep her mouth shut in a just cause, would get crushed with her.

The next day Ms. Hauser passed out dittoed sheets and told them to follow along while she read to them. What she'd chosen for her audience was Robert Frost's "Birches" about a boy's pleasure swinging on birch trees. There was also a short poem about broken toys and a broken friendship written for adults, not children, and some simple haiku about nature.

Ms. Hauser read well. She didn't make them discuss the poems to death either. When she'd finished, all she asked was which one they'd like to hear again. "The short ones," a wise guy called out, but the class listened as quietly to the second reading as the first. Carly was impressed, both with Ms. Hauser as a teacher and with her classmates for having more sensitivity than she'd expected.

The next day, after some more reading from dittoed sheets, Ms. Hauser suggested they try writing their own poems. Carly listened wistfully as Ms. Hauser read aloud a few student-written poems, wistfully because these classmates, who had shut her out, revealed sentiments as deep as any she had heard from kids in California.

Shortly after that, the anonymous poet appeared.

"This was dropped on my desk after lunch," Ms. Hauser told them. Her eyes sparkled as she held up a paper napkin and read from it. The poem described a lake like a tear on the face of the hill with all its darkness glittering in the sunshine. "What do you think?" Ms. Hauser asked them.

The murmurs agreed that it was "nice," "pretty," "good." "I think so too," Ms. Hauser said. "I wish I knew who wrote it."

In English class the following afternoon, Carly saw Chet pluck the cash register tape from his pocket and let it fall on Ms. Hauser's desk as he passed en route to his own.

"Our anonymous poet strikes again. This one's called, 'The Sounds of Seasons,'" Ms. Hauser told the class. Then she read the back of the cash register tape aloud to them.

Spring peepers chirp in chorus all night long,
Summer is rustling wind and hooting owl,
Fall brings the grating buzz of katydids and crickets.
Winter is silent.

Carly got out of English class first because she sat in front. She waited for Chet in the hall and said quietly, "I don't see how you can write poetry like that and want to kill deer."

"What?" he asked.

"You're the anonymous poet. How can you be a nature lover without feeling anything for that buck?"

"You're a pest, you know that?"

"Will you meet me at the deer stand so we can talk about it? Please?"

He hesitated and muttered, "I don't know. I'll see."

"Come today," she begged his retreating back. She couldn't be sure she'd changed the deers' habits, and even if she had, why not enlist Chet on her side against the hunters? Judging by his poetry, he *had* to be on her side.

*

Carly waited anxiously on the platform, not at all sure Chet would really come. The air was full of flying leaves, and the wind sang nasally through the evergreens, first to one side of her and then to the other, a stop and a crescendo. Two crows cawed as they flew by, but the deer weren't around.

Carly tried to prepare her arguments. What would convince him? It seemed so obvious that if he loved beautiful things, he must love the buck, and if he loved the buck, he couldn't kill it. It would make him feel rotten to kill it. He owed it to himself to be on the buck's side.

She took Chet's arrival as a sign that she'd win.

"Well, I'm here," he said and settled himself with his legs dangling over the edge of the platform and his back toward her.

She was sitting cross-legged with her back against the tree, but she moved next to him and dangled her legs too. Talking to his face had to be more effective than talking to his back.

"So, how many deer have you killed so far?" she began briskly.

"None."

"*None?* Then how do you know you'd like it?"

"I like hunting."

"Making something dead?"

"Listen, venison is good eating just the way a steer or a calf or a lamb or a pig or a chicken is. A deer is an animal."

"So is a man."

"Right, but we happen to be at the top of the heap. Everything eats something else in nature, and we have to eat too."

"We don't *have* to. My aunt and uncle are vegetarians."

"Are you a vegetarian?"

"Here I am, because they are, and I don't miss eating meat."

"Yeah, well, for my taste, nothing's better than a nice thick charcoal-grilled hamburger with ketchup and maybe a thick slice of onion. Yum. My mouth's watering just thinking about it."

"Listen," she said. "I don't care what you eat so long as you don't shoot my deer."

"Okay." He settled into the argument. "Suppose you were a farm kid and had a pet calf you'd raised yourself, or maybe a pig. You'd feel bad when it got big enough to be slaughtered, but you'd get used to it because that's the way life is, right?"

"And would I be expected to shoot my pet calf my-self?"

He sighed. "All right, think about it this way. A hunter works hard to put meat on the table. It's more honest than going to the supermarket for plastic-wrapped meat somebody else has killed. You give the animal a fair chance when you're hunting it."

"Which makes you feel better, a hunk of venison or the sight of a live deer in the woods?"

"The vension, if I'm hungry enough."

"Don't give me that, Chet. You're not starving. Your family's not poor."

He snorted. "My father's not bringing in enough to cover the bills; so I guess we're getting there."

"Deer meat isn't free," she pointed out. "Guns and hunting licenses cost money."

He rubbed his cheek. "I should've known better than to come and try to argue with you. You're too smart . . . . Look, chances are nobody'll even see your buck when deer season starts."

"Promise me that if you see him, you won't shoot him."

"Why? I'm not the only guy who's going to be out hunting."

"I know." Her voice trembled. "I can't save him from everybody, but just—please, Chet, you couldn't write poems about natural beauty if you didn't love it. And it means a lot to me that you not be the one."

He looked at her. She looked right back. In a good cause, she had no shame. His eyes softened and he asked the first personal question he'd ever asked her. "Why'd you come to live with your aunt and uncle anyway? I mean, how come you didn't stay with your father?"

"Because . . . because my father isn't what I thought he was."

"What do you mean?"

"I thought he was loving and good, and he's not."

"What'd he do to you?"

"He didn't do anything to me. It was my mother he was rotten to."

"So how long are you going to stay here?"

"As long as my aunt and uncle will put up with me probably."

"You're a funny girl. I can't figure you out."

She was glad to think he'd spent time trying and assured him cheerfully, "I'm really a very nice person when you get to know me."

"Really" he mimicked as if she'd amused him. He swung his legs which were weighted with the heavy work boots he always wore. His jacket smelled faintly of wood smoke, and he bulked large beside her, but the curve of his cheek was as soft as a girl's. She liked him a lot.

"Okay," he said. "I won't kill your buck."

"Promise?"

"I said it, didn't I?" He frowned at her. "I won't kill the buck even if he's the only deer I see all hunting season, and I won't drive him toward any other hunter if I recognize him."

"But you'll go hunting?"

"Come *on*," he said. "There's thousands of deer in this county. You can't protect them all."

"I wish I could."

"Well, you can't; so don't act crazy." He swung down from the platform and off the ladder.

"Hey, Chet," she called after him, and when he turned around to look, she gave him a big smile. "Thanks for coming. And thanks for what you promised."

"Yeah," he said and was gone.

A tree branch cracked in the wind and fell. He liked her too. He wouldn't have promised her anything if he hadn't liked her. Her smile lasted all the way back to Lu and Ben's house.

9

Lu commented that Carly seemed happier lately. Carly looked up from the chessboard on which she and Ben were playing and said, "That's because I've finally made a friend."

"You have? Good," Lu said. "How come you haven't invited her over yet?"

"It's Chet. And I've *asked* him to come over but he keeps telling me he's busy. I think it embarrasses him to be friends with a girl. Like it ruins his he-man image."

Ben moved a pawn and said, "Chet's probably shy. Most boys his age are."

"Girls, too," Lu said. "In fact, you're the only nonshy thirteen-year-old I've ever met, Carly."

"Well, I've been practicing lowering my eyes and mumbling 'I dunno,' so I'll fit in better," Carly joked, except it wasn't altogether a joke.

"And does dimming the high beams work for you?" Ben asked her.

"What?" Lu asked him, but Carly understood what he meant and nodded. She was indeed trying for less flash, and it seemed to her that her classmates weren't turning their backs on her and withdrawing anymore.

*

Outside Carly's homeroom window, a band of fading amber and russet leaves separated immaculate blue sky and tawny grass field. While she idly considered whether the colors were more or less pleasing than when they'd blazed brighter in early October, she missed most of the principal's announcement over the intercom.

"What's an environmental clean-up day?" she asked the classroom at large. Answers came from every direction. It was a garbage pick-up day, a fun day outdoors, a way to earn money for the eighth grade dance by finding deposit bottles. It was the principal's pet project left over from when he'd been a teacher in the sixties. In any case, it was a half day out of the classroom and what could be better in this Indian summer weather?

Friday morning she arrived at school with the plastic lawn-and-leaf bags everyone was supposed to bring and discovered Chet was to be her partner. She beamed at him. He frowned. "Mrs. Pit's paired everybody off," he told Carly quickly, in case she thought he'd chosen her.

"So what do we do?" she asked him, undismayed.

"They drive us to where they want us to collect garbage and pick us up farther up the road a couple of hours later. Any deposit bottles or cans we find go toward the eighth grade party."

"Sounds efficient."

"Yeah. The town roads look good for about a week after clean-up day. Then they're a mess again till next year."

Their class was assigned to a dump truck. Carly climbed the ramp into the open back and stood jammed in together with her holiday-spirited classmates. They were probably in violation of the state seat belt laws, but who cared!

A moon-faced girl Carly recognized from her lunchtimes in the art room said to her, "Aren't we lucky with the weather? Last year it rained and the truck forgot to pick up me and my partner. Boy, did we get soaked!"

"One of these big plastic bags would've made a good raincoat," Carly said.

"We didn't think of *that*. You're so clever," the girl said.

"I just don't like being cold and wet," Carly said quickly. She'd learned that being called clever here was more of an accusation than a compliment. "Did you find a lot of bottles last year?"

"Some, but the eighth graders always get the best spots because they're allowed a live band if they collect enough. You know, for their party? I'm glad we're eighth graders this year. I hope we bring in a million bottles."

"Are you going to the party?" Carly tried to hide her surprise that a boy would invite this girl. She wasn't very attractive with her round face, flat features and the roll of fat bulging over her jeans.

"Everybody goes. There's games if you don't dance," the girl said.

"Sounds like fun," Carly said, but she expected that the most popular girls went with boys anyway.

Chet was wedged into a group of rowdy boys near the tailgate, as far away from Carly as he could get, but when the truck stopped at the beginning of a steep mountain road, and the teacher in charge read off her name and his, he was obliged to get off alone with her.

"Hey, hey, hey, don't get lost in the woods you two," one of the boys in Chet's group yelled as Carly jumped off the tailgate with her plastic bags in hand.

"Pick you up at the overlook around eleven," the teacher said. The truck groaned loudly, gearing down to climb the hill.

Across the macadam road, gray cliffs of blasted rock rose straight up. Spray painted declarations of love or simple records of names and dates defaced the boulders below the cliffs. Chet and Carly stood on a grassy verge on their side of the road. Past it, the valley opened out below them with a lake and toy-sized farm buildings scattered through it. More mountains made fuzzy gray humps beyond the valley.

"What a beautiful view!" Carly said.

Chet glanced at the vista and asked, "You want to hold the bag open while I pick up, or you want to work your own bag?"

She smiled up at him. "Let's work together. That way we can talk."

"What about?"

"I'll think of something."

"Yeah," he said. "I guess you will."

"You think I talk too much?"

"I didn't say that." His sudden grin appeased her. "We going to fight or pick up trash?"

"The thing is," she explained, "I never know where I *stand* with you. You're always so critical of me."

"I am not." He looked appalled. "I think you're fine."

"You do?"

He grimaced. "Okay, you got me to say it. Now let's get to work." He picked up a plastic sandwich bag and a rusted piece of tail pipe and dropped them in the shiny black bag before handing it to her.

She held the bag open and kept pace with him as he moved toward some beer cans. "I think it's disgusting that people mess up the countryside with graffiti," she said pointing at one glaring example of bad taste. The name "Miki" was scrawled in two-foot-high drippy red letters on a rock face that stood out grandly against the sky.

"Yeah, it is," he said.

"Hey, we agree on something!" she said.

He pitched a dead sneaker and an empty box into the open maw of the plastic bag, then shook open a second bag from the box she had contributed and put the beer cans into it.

"Funny, the things people toss out of their cars," he said. "I found a shoe box once with a new pair of shoes in it."

"Did they fit?"

"Open-toed, high-heeled sandals aren't my style," he said straight-faced. "I figure some guy got mad at his wife and threw her fancy party shoes out the window."

Carly laughed. "Or those shoes killed some lady's feet and the store wouldn't take them back; so she threw them away in a temper on the way home."

"Or they fell off the back of a delivery truck."

"I give up," she said, having lost interest in the game. She started talking about the deer, about how she was feeding them every night. "It's really something to see them in the moonlight," she said. "You ought to come over some night and I'll show you."

"Maybe," he said.

A rabbit started from a patch of grass and scissored off into the rocks. His white tail whisked the grass tops. Rather than push Chet too hard, Carly changed subjects. "You and your father get enough wood in for winter?" she asked. She had noted the local preoccupation with wood chopping. Most people heated with wood stoves to save fuel bills.

"We're getting there. He's even talking of cutting some to sell."

"Still no work?"

"Not enough."

"Is he grouchy?"

"Pop doesn't get grouchy, just quiet. He's a pretty sociable guy, and when he gives up his bowling night and goes off in the woods alone for no reason, we know he's worried."

"Maybe he ought to advertise, you know, offer a special on enclosing the porch or finishing off an attic before winter."

"That's not how it's done around here."

"So how is it done then?"

"Word of mouth. . . . He could build a cabin on speculation for the summer people if he can get the bank to give him a loan."

"And will he?"

"He's thinking about it. Pop doesn't like to owe money."

Chet's unclouded admiration for his father irked her. "I used to think my father was perfect too," she said. "I even had a girl friend who was so crazy about him she pretended that he was her dad. And her father wasn't *bad*, just dull." Carly picked up a soda bottle he'd missed in the weeds and handed it to him for the bottle bag.

"I don't think Pop's perfect," Chet said. "I just like the way he is."

"Do you like the way your mother is?"

"My mother's okay." He sounded a shade defensive.

"My mother was sweet-tempered," Carly offered. "She never got mad and yelled the way my father and I do. Probably she'd have been better off if she had lost her temper at us once in a while, especially with my father."

101

Carly was so intent on what she was saying, she walked right past a cache of beer cans which Chet pounced on with a gleeful shout. She didn't even know if he was listening to her, but she continued talking about her father anyway. "Dad doesn't have a conscience about what he can get away with unless you make him see he's being selfish. *I* never let him get away with anything. 'You *have* to come to my dance recital or I won't perform,' I'd tell him, and he'd come, even if he had business to do—if it was for me."

"A girl's closer to her mother, I guess," Chet said.

"Not me. I was always Daddy's girl. Always, until my mother got cancer." She waited, but he didn't comment, and a thought struck her. "Hey," she said, "I bet I know the real reason you hunt. It's because your father loves to, isn't it?"

"Lots of people around here live for the hunting season. I could tell you a million hunting stories, some funny and some pretty crazy too."

"So go ahead," she encouraged him.

"Well, for instance," he said, "one reason my father thinks my brother Joe's smart is because one time they were hunting, and these other guys who were supposed to be in on the drive didn't show up. So my father's ready to go home and try again some other day, but Joe says they don't need the other guys and for Pop just to stand and he'll drive the deer toward him all by himself."

Chet stuffed another beer can in the bag as he continued. "See, usually it takes at least a couple of hunters to drive a deer, but my father didn't want to hurt Joe's feelings because—well, Joe's touchy because he's so short. So Pop stands and waits where the deer should come out if Joe could drive it and by and by, Pop hears something. But it sounds like three guys coming. Then sure enough, the deer comes bounding through the break and my father shoots it. Turned out, Joe had his slingshot with him, and he shot stones to one side and the other as he came through the woods. So the deer thought three people were after it and didn't try to double back to get around them."

"And *that's* why your father thinks Joe's a genius, for *that?*"

"Joe's smart and hardworking. My father's going to pay his way through engineering school. Joe'll make a good engineer."

"What about you?"

"I'll go into building with Pop."

"But how can you? There's no work around even for him alone."

"That's now. Things change. Pop used to do okay .... Part of his problem is he doesn't charge people enough."

"And you would?"

"I don't know." Chet grinned, then got his mischievous look. "I can be pretty hard-nosed when I need to be."

"I'll bet!" she jeered.

"Think I'm a softie, do you?" He grabbed her arm and twisted it behind her back.

"Hey, that hurts," she complained.

"Told you I can be hard." He let her go.

She rubbed her arm, although he hadn't really hurt her. "You should have had some sisters," she said. "Then you'd know not to do that to a girl."

"If you were a country girl, you wouldn't mind."

"Oh, wouldn't I?"

"Trouble with you is you don't understand how things are and you're too impatient to learn. You want to tell everybody how you think it should be."

"See how you criticize me all the time?"

Chet glanced at her and then away and said, "I guess you can't help yourself. You're just different. City folks are different."

"That's silly," she said. "This isn't a foreign country."

"I guess it is, in a way," he countered.

For a while they picked up trash in silence. The bag was heavy now, and he took it from her and gave her the lighter deposit-container bag instead. They were halfway up the mountain. Despite the moderate temperature, Carly was hot. "I wish we had something to drink," she said.

"What some water?" He offered her a canteen he had attached to his belt.

She took a sip and thanked him. "You know what gets me is that I like you a lot," she said. "I don't mean

104

just you personally, but the kids in class. Even if I do seem different, I don't understand why people don't like me back."

"Who said we don't? Everybody likes you pretty much."

Even though he had phrased it in a general way, his response was positive. She perked up and let the subject drop. "Did I tell you I met your brother, Joe?" she said. "He wasn't very nice to me. Did he say anything about it? It was in the apple orchard."

"Joe doesn't talk to me much."

"How come?"

"Well, he thinks my father favors me. Joe's got a chip on his shoulder about his size. My father says Joe takes after his family, and the rest of us take after my mother's."

"Your mother's not that tall."

"No, but all her brothers were and her father. See, my father used to hang out with her brothers. Mom says he only married her to become part of her family because he admires them so much."

"Joe was shooting his gun in the apple orchard."

"He likes shooting."

"I'd hate it if I had a brother I didn't get along with," she said. "I guess I'm lucky I'm the only child."

"That's not lucky. Come Christmas when everybody gets home, our house is a three-ring circus. I wouldn't want to miss that."

"That's funny," she said. "I thought you were the loner and I was the one who needed people around."

"Well, sometimes I enjoy being alone, like in the woods. I like it when it's so quiet that every sound means something. I like when the wind sort of talks to me."

"What you should be is a poet," she said.

He laughed. "No way. I'm going to work with my hands."

They had reached the top of the hill. The rest area, where the next pair of eighth graders had been dropped off, had already been cleared out. "We might as well sit here and wait for the truck to come around for us," Chet said. He settled onto the lone picnic table with the trash bag on the ground beside him.

She hoisted herself up next to him and held her face up to the sun. "I love sunshine," she said.

"So what kind of things did you do out in California?" he asked, "I mean for fun."

"Well—" She considered. She didn't want to put him off altogether by telling him about her dancing lessons and the concerts and recitals and art shows to which she and her mother had gone. "I went to the movies a lot."

"Um," he said.

"And my father and I went camping usually for a few days in the fall. Sometimes we went to the beach. And my friends and I had parties at each other's houses, and we'd hang out at the local taco stand and go roller-skating at the rink sometimes."

He nodded. "Doesn't sound too bad."

"There's more to do in the city than around here."

"Depends on what you like to do."

"True, if you want to go around shooting animals, it's better here."

"You never give up, do you?" He sounded disgusted.

She didn't answer him. Her determination was one of the things her father admired about her. "My little girl's got guts," he'd boasted to the policeman who had pulled him out of the car wreck before it exploded. She'd gone for help, then come back and refused to leave his side until help came. "My superdaughter," he'd called her. Now Chet was disliking the very characteristic her father found so wonderful. Unless Dad had changed his mind by now. Dad might not be liking her so much anymore either. He hadn't called or written in a while.

She and Chet had been the first to be dropped off, and they were the first the truck picked up on its second go-around. Chet slid down and leaned his back against the truck's side. Boldly, she slid down next to him and was relieved that he didn't move away. Even when the others joined them, two by two, he didn't shift position.

"Get a lot of deposits?" they were asked. Some kids had collected much more than they had, but nonetheless, Carly was very satisfied with her morning's profits.

They had lunch back in school where everyone seemed more interested in hearing what the total of all the deposit cans and bottles they'd collected came to than in resuming schoolwork. The announcement of the eighth graders' earnings brought a cheer from Carly's math class. Along with the bake sale monies and the contribution from the Parent–Teacher's Organization, they now had enough for a three-piece band for the eighth grade party.

"Are you going to the party, Chet?" Carly turned around in her seat to ask him.

"Maybe," he said. But he didn't invite her to go with him.

Patience, she advised herself. Patience was the only way to win with Chet.

10

"I don't know," Lu said to Carly as they sat on the couch playing Scrabble. "If I were going to that eighth grade party, I'd want something new to wear."

"I haven't made up my mind whether to go or not, Lu, and I really hate shopping," Carly said.

Her mother had held to certain shopping principles. She wouldn't buy anything that wasn't top quality, well fitting, flattering, and on sale besides. They'd gone home empty-handed and exhausted too many times. "It's funny," Carly said while she waited for Lu to make a word from her bad mix of letters. "I only found out Mother really *enjoyed* those trips to the mall when she was in the hospital and she mentioned—" Carly stopped talking, too choked up suddenly to continue. Mother had been so wistful when she'd wondered aloud if they would ever go shopping together again.

"You and your mother were very different, weren't you?" Lu asked.

"Very," Carly said. "Mother was too nice. She never complained, and she was *so* grateful when you did something for her. Not that I did much until after she got sick."

"Drastic situations sometimes bring out our best behavior," Lu said. She attached the word *sty* going down from the end of the word *axe* for twenty-three points.

"*You* behave well all the time," Carly said.

"Oh, come on, Carly. You've lived with us long enough to know better. Don't I get on Ben's nerves when I'm careless and sloppy about the house?"

Carly laughed. "You do, but that's his fault for being so fussy. I mean, who cares whether you remember to close the kitchen cabinets or screw on a bottle cap crooked?"

"He does, and for his sake, I should try to change my bad habits."

"I guess."

"Do you ever feel guilty for not having been a perfect daughter to your mother?" Lu asked.

"Yes," Carly said. "Yes, I do a lot."

"I did too after I lost my parents. I think it's normal to think of all the things you should have done when it's too late to do anything about them."

Carly considered. "Except—some people have more to regret than others." She studied her letters. If she only had an *e*, she'd have a seven-letter word.

"Would you go to the party if Chet invited you to go with him?" Lu asked.

"But he didn't invite me," Carly said. "You wouldn't go alone, would you if you were me? I could end up being shut out by everyone and come home ready to kill myself."

"But Chet will be there, and he'll talk to you."

"Who knows? If he wanted to spend the evening with me, he'd ask me to go with him. Lots of kids are going as couples, and the rest will hang around with their friends."

"Umm," Lu said. "You can't even pretend to be having a good time if you're standing by yourself at a party."

"You've got it," Carly said. "So would you take a chance?"

"I wasn't much of a risk taker at your age," Lu said. "I'd probably have stayed home with a good book. But you're braver than I was."

Carly added a *d* to *equate* and used her *z* on a triple letter, scoring fifty points which evened their scores.

"Terrific," Lu said. "You're such a good player." She reassembled her letters and said thoughtfully, "You know, you just might have a better chance to make friends with *girls* at a party. They'll be insecure there and maybe freer to talk to you. But don't go on my say-so. I'd feel terrible if it was a bust."

Suddenly Carly decided. Not to go would make her feel like a coward, and she wasn't that. "I guess I'll go," she said. "Why not?" While she was at it, she even agreed to go shopping with Lu.

Friday night they set off for the mall. Ben stayed home, claiming to be even more allergic to shopping that Carly was.

Lu made a good mall companion. She ambled along looking at merchandise and other shoppers as if they were in an amusement park rather than on a treasure hunt. Carly stopped to sift through a table of brightly colored T-shirts and casually selected two that would do. "This is fun," Carly said as they waited at the cash register for the salesgirl to wrap her purchase.

"I like to shop once in a while," Lu admitted as if it were a vice. "I'm not quite the anticonsumer Ben is, but don't you tell him that."

Carly laughed and said, "Your secret is safe with me."

The blouse she bought for the party was high-necked with lace inserts and long sleeves. Chet had never seen her in anything feminine. She wondered if he'd like it. In her usual shirts and pants, she could have passed for a slight young boy if her face weren't so pert and delicate boned. "Cute" was the compliment people gave her. She'd rather have had long black hair, long legs, and a bust. That might be Chet's preference too, for all she knew. "Should I wear makeup?" Carly asked Lu.

"For Chet? Hard to say," Lu said. "You'd look older with makeup, but it might frighten him off altogether."

"Ummm. Probably the blouse's enough."

*

The girl in the mirror looked appealing to Carly on

the night of the party. Daringly, she darkened her eye-lashes with mascara and touched her lips with gloss.

Ben whistled when she came downstairs and he said, "Wow, do you look pretty!"

Carly gasped. "I forgot to feed the deer!"

"No sweat," Ben said agreeably. "I'll do it for you."

He lugged out the apples and scattered them. Afterward he and Lu dropped Carly off in front of the brightly lighted school. Dancing was to be in the cafeteria. Games were set up in the hall and the gym. Carly could hear the three-piece band tuning up.

"We'll pick you up at ten. Have fun," Ben said.

Carly couldn't resist kissing him. "You're so nice," she said. For good measure she kissed Lu too.

"Good luck," Lu called after her as Carly ran toward the entrance.

Her heart was bouncing with excitement. She recognized the thick blond braid of the girl ahead of her in the ticket line and said, "Hi, Megan."

The girl turned around. "Oh, hi, Carly. Are you here by yourself too?"

"Uh-huh."

"My friend Nadine was supposed to come with me, but she got sick. I hate going in alone. How about you and me standing together?"

"Sure," Carly said gladly. "You look nice, Megan. That's a pretty sweater."

"It's my sister's. She said I could wear it if I didn't drink anything I could spill on it, but I'm so nervous

113

I'm sweating. Lucky she didn't say anything about sweating." Megan giggled.

"The band sounds pretty good," Carly said.

"My brother's in it." Megan sounded pleased. "Do you play an instrument?"

"Just the guitar a little," Carly said.

"Really? I play the piano. Want to come to my house sometime and see how we do together?"

"That'd be fun," Carly said. "When?"

"Oh, soon," Megan said vaguely.

Once inside she led Carly toward a circle of five girls near the refreshment table. The girls were having an animated conversation about whether anybody was going to try to sneak liquor into the party the way last year's eighth graders had. To Carly's relief, Megan included her in the circle too. Across the vast empty space between the refreshment table and the band, Carly saw Chet. He was standing with two of his friends, arms folded, watching the action, or the nonaction. Nobody was dancing.

"Where is everybody?" Carly asked.

"Outside in the hall playing games," a girl answered her and added, "Last year nobody started to dance until it was time to go home."

"But we're in eighth grade now," another girl said hopefully. "The boys aren't such babies anymore."

"How about we invite the boys to dance?" Carly asked. She loved dancing and couldn't wait to get out on the floor.

"Go ahead. You try it," the second girl was quick to dare her.

"Not by myself." Carly could just imagine Chet's reaction if she asked him to join her on that vacant dance floor. He'd faint from shock.

"We could go play games," Megan said unenthusiastically.

"Or we could give the boys the idea by dancing with each other," Carly said.

"Who's going to start?" the eager girl asked.

Carly began stepping to the beat of the music. "Let's all do it together," she said as she put her arms and shoulders into it. For an instant the girls froze, watching her. Then Megan started shyly going with the rhythm, and as if that was the signal, the others in the circle began dancing too.

Two of them broke off and danced facing each other. Another girl ran across the room and skidded into the circle to join them. Then a boy jumped into the middle and began jigging around, clowning, but dancing nevertheless. The band kept the number going on and on, as if to encourage them now that they were finally responding to the music. By the time the music stopped, some boys were out on the floor, and the group had broken up into couples.

At the start of the next number, Carly saw Chet watching her. He was still making like a statue. Deliberately she walked over to him. "The music's good, isn't it?" she asked.

"Yeah."

"So how come you're not dancing?"

"Nobody's asked me," he said.

"Will you dance with me?"

He looked trapped and foolish. "Come on," he mumbled and took her hand to walk her into the midst of the dancers. Camouflage, she thought and grinned as he faced her and began moving. He was a little awkward, but not as bad as some of the other boys who looked as if they were stomping on hornets.

The music ended, but Chet stayed with her. They danced again, and when the band took a break, he asked, "Want to go try some games?"

"Okay," she said casually so that he wouldn't guess how delighted she was that he hadn't walked away from her. "But let's stop for refreshments."

His thirst amused her, and the speedy way he helped doughnuts disappear from the pile on a tray.

They played Fooz ball. She was quick to block the ball and twist her little mechanical man to kick it back, but Chet was quicker and won the game. Next she had her fortune told. Chet shook his head when the girl with exaggerated makeup, satiny-looking blouse and skirt like a gypsy's reached for his hand. "No, thanks," he said.

"Are you superstitious?" Carly asked him.

"No, but that stuff is just junk. She doesn't know anything."

Carly was quiet as they moved along to the electronic games past the Ping-Pong table. She knew the "gypsy" was just a girl with no special vision of the future, but it had given her a chill to be told she was going on a long journey soon and that she would have three husbands. "I don't want three husbands," she told Chet.

"You're too young to have any," he said reasonably.

"I won't be young for long." The sad truth of that struck her hard.

He looked at her curiously. "Listen, you'll do all right."

"I will?"

"Sure," he said, and though he had no more ability to see the future than her fortune-teller had, she felt relieved.

They were standing near the door of the gym when the band started up again. A boy hurrying into the room bumped into Carly and asked, "Hey, want to dance with me?"

She looked at Chet who pointedly looked away from her. "Do you mind?" she asked Chet. She thought it would be wise not to hang around him all evening anyway.

"I don't care," he mumbled.

The boy was an excellent dancer, more interested in her as a partner than as a person. "You really know the moves," he told her.

"Thanks. You're not so bad yourself."

117

They danced and it was fun, but when the music stopped and he dashed off, she looked around to find that Chet had disappeared. She wondered if she'd made a mistake. Taking another partner set him free, but had he felt rejected? Uneasily, she returned to the refreshment table and stood watching the dance floor, wishing she had more experience in dealing with boys.

"We're going to the girls' room. Want to come?" Megan said.

"Sure," Carly agreed gladly.

When Carly came out she was asked to dance again and soon after, the evening was over. "It was so short," she complained.

"Short and sweet," Megan said. "Didn't you have a good time?"

"Oh, yes, I really did," Carly said.

"Want to bring your guitar over to my house Saturday?"

"Sure," Carly said, "if I can get a ride." They exchanged telephone numbers outside where the hall lights shone behind them. Then Megan's father tooted his horn and she ran. Carly saw Chet go up to his father's panel truck. Joe was sitting in it beside Harry. Chet started to get in, but Harry said something, and with apparent reluctance, Chet turned around and walked back toward her.

"Your aunt called and asked Pop to bring you home. Their car broke down," Chet said.

"Oh. Okay."

Small as she was, she couldn't fit on the seat with the three men. "Guess you got your choice of laps," Harry said, "Joe's or Chet's."

Joe grinned at her as if he expected her to be embarrassed. "Do you mind, Chet?" she asked. Wordlessly, he sat down and helped her up on his legs.

"Now, don't that look cute," Joe said. "Bet that's the first time Chet's ever had a girl in his arms."

"I'm not in his arms; I'm on his lap," Carly said tartly.

"Better watch out for this one, Joe," Harry said. "She's got a quick tongue."

"I already caught some of it," Joe said. "She objected to my shooting at crows in our own orchard."

"Is that what you were shooting at?" she asked. Joe smelled of beer. He was only in high school. Carly wondered where he'd gotten it and whether Harry minded. "Have you been to a party too, Joe?"

"Bowling with my pop. Tonight's his regular bowling night," Joe said.

"Joe did real good. He got three strikes in a row."

Joe laughed. "You weren't so bad yourself."

"Are you a good bowler too?" Carly asked Chet.

"No," he said shortly, looking out the window as if he weren't part of the conversation.

"What Chet's best at is eating," Joe said.

"He's a growing boy," Harry defended his youngest.

"Chet said you're going to be an engineer," Carly offered in an attempt to reach Joe's nice spot—if he had any.

119

"*I* didn't know Chet could talk," Joe said with feigned surprise. "Thought all he did was eat and grunt. I guess it takes a girl to bring him out. There's nothing like a female for talking, of course."

"You're a pretty good talker yourself, Joe," Harry put in, and answered Carly's question obliquely. "Yeah, Joe's the brains in the family."

"Why engineering? Why not medicine or law?" she asked Joe and finally got a straight answer from him.

"Because," Joe said, "I like dealing with practical stuff like machinery and fixing things, and I don't like sick people; so I'd never make a doctor."

"You're good enough with words to be a lawyer," Harry said.

"Something wrong with engineering?" Joe asked Carly.

"She's just contentious," Harry said. "This little girl will argue about anything. Last time it was hunting. She don't think we should be hunting the whitetail. Thinks it's cruel to shoot them. Right, Carly?"

She refused to be baited. "Right," she said flatly.

"City girl," Joe said with a grin.

Despite herself, Carly began arguing, "We ought to preserve the beautiful things in this world."

"Now there you got the right idea," Joe said. "That's just what hunters do. They preserve the natural beauty of the deer by killing them quick and easy instead of letting them starve to death. You want to see something pitiful, come around after a real hard winter and see deer stumbling along barely able to stand up, with their ribs showing and their hides all worn."

"Instead of shooting them, why couldn't you *feed* them in the winter?" Carly asked.

"Because, city girl, we got a few other things to do around here," Joe answered.

"One winter," Harry began conversationally, "I cut down a whole bunch of saplings so the deer could reach the tender parts, the tips, you know. But we'd have had to take down half the woods to make a difference that winter. Must've had six feet of snow in places. Winters like that the deer gather in yards, bare spots in the woods they've pretty well cleared, and when the food's gone there, they just starve to death."

"Or the wild dogs get them," Joe put in.

"Right," Harry said. "Deer can outrun the dogs except in deep snow. Then the dogs chase 'em until the deer drop of exhaustion, or the dogs will force a deer out onto an icy lake where its hooves slip. Once the deer goes down, the dogs attack without fear of being kicked. Those powerful forefeet is all the protection the bucks have in late winter after their antlers drop off."

"There must be some way to help them," Carly insisted, against the force of Harry's argument. "Cattle are kept alive over the winter. Couldn't the state pay to feed the deer hay or whatever?"

"But then the dumb deer just keep multiplying," Joe said. "What do you want to do, pack the woods with pet deer that aren't any good to anybody? Where are you going to find the tax money to do that?"

"But there has to be some solution," Carly cried.

Harry chuckled and said, "There is—hunting."

"No," she said.

"You think about it, you'll see hunting's the fairest way," Harry said. He tooted his horn at a car that burned rubber passing him on the country road.

"Not for my deer, not mine," Carly murmured to Chet while Harry gave the long-gone driver a hefty piece of his mind.

Chet met her eyes briefly.

"You promised," she said softly.

He nodded.

"Thank you for the ride," she told Harry when he let her off at the A-frame.

"My pleasure," Harry said. "Tell your aunt, 'Anytime.'" He waved and drove off.

Lu looked up when Carly walked into the house. She'd been lying on the couch reading. "How did it go, honey?"

"Fine," Carly said.

"You don't sound so fine."

"It was all right." Carly sat down next to Lu and propped her chin on her fists. "I danced with Chet and some other boys and I got invited to a girl's house, but—"

"But what? That sounds like a success story."

"I can't stand Chet's brother Joe. He's obnoxious and Chet's father kind of plays both sides. First he puts in something for Chet, and then switches over and throws in a word for Joe. He acts nice, and what he said about hunting makes sense in a way, but he'll never change my mind about my buck."

"You ran into complications, huh?"

"Shooting deer just can't be right," Carly said passionately. "There *has* to be a better way."

Lu smoothed the hair back from Carly's forehead without saying anything.

"Well, what do *you* think?" Carly asked her.

"I know what you mean. I guess I just don't get as emotional about contradictory situations as you do. I'm glad Ben doesn't hunt, and I wouldn't shoot a wild animal except in self-defense myself, but if other people want to, that's their business."

"My beautiful little buck is so new to the world," Carly said. "Surely there's a place in it for him."

She went to bed depressed, and a bad case of the purple pain kept her from falling asleep until nearly dawn.

11

Everything was improving and Carly couldn't understand why the purple pain kept erupting and suffocating her in hot lava. It was so bad on the Monday morning after the dance that she couldn't get herself out of bed.

"I'm not feeling well," she told Lu who had come into her room to see why she wasn't up yet.

"Do you think you have a fever?" Lu promptly felt Carly's forehead.

"I don't think I'm that kind of sick," Carly told her anxious aunt. "I just don't feel like moving."

"Want me to stay home and keep you company?"

"No, thanks, Lu." Carly was touched by her aunt's concern, but what she wanted was to be alone. She slept off and on all morning, and in between sleeping she wept. The weeping seemed excessive to her, but she couldn't control it.

She'd prepared for her mother's death by reading books on death and coping with loss. The books talked about delayed reactions, which was what she supposed she was having.

Strangely though, it wasn't her mother she was thinking about, but her father. Images kept turning up in her mind of sailing adventures with him, dinner conversations when she and he had scrapped happily over whose football team was going to win the championship or whether it was okay to use animals in laboratory experiments for the eventual benefit of humans. Most disconcerting of all, Carly couldn't remember her mother's face. She got out of bed to find the picture she carried in her wallet of a young, smiling, healthy woman. "Mother," Carly said out loud, but the picture remained only vaguely familiar.

Deliberately Carly concentrated. Thirteen years of living with someone had to leave memories, even bad things, anything. She went over the checklist of what had been— the mother-daughter concert and museum trips, shopping and lunches out. Finally, she did recall a scene. She'd been ill and her mother had tried to read to her, but Carly had asked to be left alone. "You're just like your father," Mother had said bitterly. "He never wants me around when he's sick either."

What a mean kid she'd been, Carly thought. Instead of appreciating her mother's devotion, she'd found it as suffocating as heavy perfume in a crowded elevator.

"She's too icky," Carly had told her father once.

"Your mother's a sweet lady," he'd said. "Aren't you a sweet little girl?"

125

"Not me. I take after you," Carly had told him with pride, and when he laughed, she had laughed with him.

*

Tuesday morning Carly woke up hanging on to the tail end of a dream about her father. She missed him. She couldn't help herself. She missed him a lot. Forlornly, she got out of bed and dressed.

"Feeling better?" Ben asked her at breakfast.

"I'm fine."

Megan greeted her warmly in school. "Were you sick?" she asked. "I was going to call you if you didn't come today."

"Were you?" Carly smiled. "That's nice. I'm fine. What did I miss?"

"The principal complimented our class on how well we behaved at the party," Megan said with pride.

"Good," Carly said. "We should ask him to let us have another one soon."

"Hey, that's an idea," Megan said. "I wonder if he would. That's a really great idea. . . . Don't forget you're coming over to my house Saturday. Right?"

"Right," Carly said.

Chet returned her greeting with an eyes-down mumble. At the end of homeroom, she turned around to ask him quietly, "Is something wrong? Are you mad at me?"

"No."

"You are," she said. "What is it? You mad because I argued with your father and brother on the way home from the dance?"

126

He gave her a funny look. "I didn't care about that."

"Oh," she said. "You're mad at me for something else?"

The tightness went out of his expression. "Forget it," he said. Whatever his grudge against her had been, he was giving it up. "It's okay."

"Then will you come over this afternoon? We could do our homework together."

He half laughed, shaking his head, as if she were altogether too much for him. "Okay," he said. "If my father doesn't need me, I'll come."

She found another one-page letter from her father when she got home from school. ". . . Some friends of mine have invited me to spend Christmas in Hawaii with them. If you're still planning to be ticked off at me by then, I'll go, although I'd rather be with you. Just say the word and I'll make reservations for us someplace like Vail where we could ski. In any case, I want to hear from you immediately. You may as well know that I'm fed up with the way you're treating me. Enough is enough, Carly. . . ." He said his deal of a lifetime had fallen through, and he was taking scuba diving lessons and keeping himself busy.

She wrote to him, telling him to make whatever plans he wanted for Christmas and that she was sorry he was annoyed with her, but she couldn't help the way she felt. She told him about the deer and how anxious she was about the fast approaching hunting season. "I'm determined to save my buck somehow," she wrote. She said she was doing well in school and had made friends and settled in here. She ended by saying she was sorry his deal had fallen through.

Chet came over. Carly chattered to put him at ease. She badgered him about the homework he never did and told him how smart he was. She also plied him with hot cocoa and the zucchini bread Ben had baked.

"This is a nice house," Chet said about the A-frame. "I like that high ceiling with the beams exposed."

"My aunt and uncle are nice too," Carly said.

Chet nodded and startled her by asking, "You don't miss your father?"

"Of course I do," she blurted out. "I miss him a lot."

"Then you're going back to California soon?"

"No. I'm not planning to go back."

"I don't understand you," he said.

"I'm not very complicated, Chet."

He grinned at her warmly. "You sure of that?"

She grinned back and started talking about music. He was a woeful ignoramus about music, she discovered. "Next time you come, I'm going to make you listen to some records. I can't *believe* you've never ever heard real old English ballads."

"Pop says to watch out for any female that wants to make you over," Chet teased her.

"I'm not going to make you over, just expand you a little."

He took another slice of zucchini bread. "So long as you feed me while you're doing it, I guess I can take it."

Ben yelped indignantly when he got home and found the zucchini bread gone. "What'd you do, have a party here?"

"Chet came over. He eats a lot."

"I'll say. You better do your own baking next time." To show he meant it, Ben handed her his cookbook. Lu didn't have a cookbook because she found printed recipes inhibiting. That night Carly used the cookbook to bake a nut bread for the next session with Chet. He'd promised to watch with her at the deers' nightly apple party.

"You're feeling up again, aren't you?" Lu asked her as she tasted the sweet dough from the beaters before Carly washed them.

"Umm," Carly agreed. "Do you think Chet could have been mad at me because I danced with somebody else at the party?"

"Could be. After all, he's only a kid. It probably doesn't take much to make him lose his confidence."

*

Chet complained about the cold as he huddled on the hood of Ben's car after helping Carly toss out apples near the salt lick. "If you were hunting, you'd be willing to sit and *freeze*," she said.

"Not me," Chet said. "Tracking the deer is the part I like. Moving keeps you warm."

129

She touched his arm with her mittened hand to silence him. The buck stood twenty feet away, looking at them alertly. His antlers were elegant as Chinese writing against the pearly sky. Even in the twilight Carly could see the moist nose twitching and the brightness in the shy brown eyes. Chet swallowed. The noise sounded loud, but the buck didn't stir. Then the princely head dipped to find an apple treat.

The buck was their only guest that night. After he'd gone, Chet said, "I'd better get home for supper."

"Wasn't it wonderful?" Carly asked.

"Yeah," he agreed. "Yeah, it was nice."

When the purple pain struck her again on Friday, Carly blamed it on the weather. November was nasty. All the leaves had fallen and everything had dimmed. Gray skies hung over dull brown skeletal woods, made more sombre by the dark green of pine and spruce and cedar. The school bus passed dried out fields in shades of tan and brown and wine. Hunting season was a week off.

Carly needed a project that would absorb her and keep her from brooding. "Let's have a big Thanksgiving party," Carly suggested to her aunt. "Let's invite a whole bunch of people and make a real feast."

"Usually we go to Ben's folks for Thanksgiving, Carly."

"Couldn't we have them here?"

"Not too well. Ben has an enormous family. There'll be more than twenty people for Thanksgiving and Christmas. You're invited, of course."

"But I don't know Ben's family."

"We can't hurt their feelings, honey," Lu said apologetically. "The drive to the Berkshires is pretty and we stay overnight. It's fun."

Carly wondered if she could get herself invited to Chet's or Megan's Thanksgiving. She didn't want to meet new people. She wanted to celebrate with the ones she already knew. "I'm going over to Chet's to do homework with him tomorrow morning before I go to Megan's," Carly told Lu.

"I thought Chet didn't believe in homework," Lu said. "How're you getting him to do so much of it?"

"With difficulty," Carly said and boasted, "Actually, Chet has a hard time saying no to me."

Carly woke up early Saturday and hiked over to the Grahams' an hour before she was due. She found Chet with Joe, shooting at cans on a flat rock on the other side of the road from his house. "Want to try?" Chet asked when he saw her.

"No thanks." She wasn't about to give Joe a chance to mock her for not knowing how to handle a gun.

Chet raised the narrow rifle to his shoulder and sighted along the barrel. The shot zinged and the can bounced off the rock.

"Set it up for me," Joe said. He waited until Chet was reaching for the can, then raised the gun. Carly screamed and dropped her books when she heard the click of the empty shell being ejected, followed by a shot. It looked to her as if Joe had shot right at his brother.

131

"Watch it, you turkey, you nearly got me," Chet yelled.

Joe laughed. "Boy, did you jump! Scared, huh?"

"Dad'd be mad if he knew you aimed a gun at anyone."

"But I didn't aim at you. I wasn't within six feet of you, turkey. . . . You going to say anything to him?"

Chet shrugged.

"Maybe he won't, but *I* will," Carly said. "And I hope your father takes your rifle away for punishment."

Joe glared at her while his face turned red. "You tell him and you'll be sorry, kid," he said.

"Why? What can you do to me?"

He narrowed his eyes at her. "Hunting season starts soon, and I know a sweet little eight point buck that you like a lot."

Carly yelled, "You rat, you stinking rat. You wouldn't dare." But she suspected Joe would, and suddenly she was weeping, weeping right there in front of the two of them, a noisy flash flood of tears.

"Hey," Chet said. He patted her back gently. "Hey, it's all right. Just promise him you won't tell. Carly, you hear me?"

She heard. The torrent stopped. She wiped her eyes with the backs of her hands and looked hard at Joe. "I won't tell, but if my deer gets shot, you're going to have to shoot me too to keep me quiet."

Joe shrugged. "Nothing to get so excited about," he said. He ejected the shell from the gun and walked off toward the house with it.

132

She stood there exhausted. Chet picked up her books. "Let's go do our homework," he said. She nodded, unsurprised to find him cooperative now in an effort to soothe her.

They were working on their math at the kitchen table when Gladys came clumping down the stairs. "Told you I'd find that jacket of yours from last winter," she said to Chet. "Oh, Carly! How you doing?"

"Fine," Carly said. "How are you?"

"Not so good. The pains were so bad last night I didn't sleep a wink."

"That's too bad," Carly said.

Gladys nodded agreeably. Then she recalled the blue quilted parka in her hand. "Anyways, Chet, you can't go through the winter in that old wool shirt of your daddy's. Try this on now."

As Chet was sticking his arms into the sleeves of the parka, Joe walked into the kitchen, opened the refrigerator and asked, "Anything to eat?"

"There's some leftover chili for lunch," Gladys said absently. She was rubbing her chin at the sight of a good four inches of Chet's wrists and lower arms stretching past the cuffs of the jacket. "Joe, I want you to try this parka on for me."

"What for?"

"I just want to see something."

Grudgingly, Joe obliged. The jacket fit him fine. "Well," Gladys said. "What we can do is, you take Chet's jacket and we'll get him a bigger one."

"I'm not going to wear my little brother's old clothes."

"Joe, you know we aren't flush this year. We got to make do, and that's a good jacket Chet outgrew."

"I won't wear his crap," Joe yelled. He yanked the jacket off as if he'd like to rip it, but it didn't tear. He slammed out of the room.

Harry walked in just then. "What's going on here?"

"Joe's mad because Chet's growing and he's not," Gladys said, showing more understanding of her sons than Carly would have expected.

"Yeah, well, nothing we can do about that."

"Listen," Chet said. "How about cutting the sleeves off, and I can wear it as a vest with the wool shirt? That'd suit me fine."

"Old jacket don't fit?" Harry asked glumly.

"I'd rather have a vest, really," Chet said.

Harry grunted. "I guess I can still afford to buy my son a jacket."

It was nearly noon, and Ben had promised to pick Carly up to take her to Megan's at twelve. "You get this feller to do his homework again?" Harry asked her jovially.

"Chet's smart," she said. "Just not motivated. He could get straight A's like Joe if he wanted."

"Well, you keep motivating him and who knows," Harry said. "Listen, how about going hunting with us one day when the season starts?"

"Me?" She was amazed. "You know I hate it."

"You haven't tried it," Harry said. "You come hunting with me, and I guarantee, I'll make a convert of you."

"You fool, Harry," Gladys said. "This girl don't want to freeze off her fingers and toes waiting for a deer dumb enough to get in range of a gun."

"Come on, Gladys. If there wasn't more to it than what you're saying, how come they call hunting the sport of kings?"

"Maybe it is," Carly said, "but I'll always be on the deer's side."

"You're missing the opportunity of a lifetime, girl." Harry shrugged and then invited her to stay to lunch.

"Stay," Gladys said. "Soon as you and Chet finish up your homework, I'll put the chili on."

"I'd like to stay, but I really can't. Thanks anyway," Carly said. The chili didn't tempt her. She'd developed a distaste for meat ever since Chet had made her think of packaged meat from the supermarket and deer meat in the same category.

"You could squash your brother if you wanted," she told Chet when they were sitting side by side on the porch waiting for Ben to pick her up.

"No, I couldn't. I'm bigger than Joe, but he's tougher. Besides, I don't want to beat him."

"Why not? He's rotten to you."

"Yeah, but he's got his problems. Anyway, one of these days I'll be too big for him to mess with."

His sympathy for his brother seemed misplaced to Carly, but she didn't argue. If Joe had been her brother, she'd have fought him. She'd never have tolerated his meanness.

She was tempted, as Ben's car pulled into the space in front of the house, to give Chet a quick good-bye kiss, but she didn't dare. He might not like it. He'd never shown an inclination to kiss her. She hoped he didn't think of her as a sister. Her attraction to him was not at all brotherly.

*

At Megan's house that afternoon, Carly began talking about boys and asked Megan what she thought of Chet just to hear what Megan would say.

"Chet's just a regular boy," Megan said. "You know, a cutup. I couldn't believe he danced with you at the party. He's never paid attention to girls before. He must have a crush on you."

Apparently Megan didn't see through Chet's camouflage to the depths he had in him, Carly thought. He was full of subtle feelings and sharp perceptions. It occurred to her that of all the people she knew here, Chet might be the best one with whom to talk about her father. She couldn't talk to Lu who still saw Dad as the respected older brother she didn't know well. And Ben wouldn't listen to anything even slightly negative about her father, either because Ben thought children shouldn't be critical of their parents or out of loyalty to a fellow male. As for Megan, she didn't have enough experience

136

to understand. Chet then, Carly decided. She needed to talk to someone.

That evening Lu and Ben took Carly with them to eat at an Italian restaurant they liked. "Did you have a good time with Megan?" Lu asked.

"Sure," Carly said. "She's kind of a goody-goody, but we had fun playing music together."

"Looks as if you've managed to fit in after all," Ben said.

"I'm making a dent," Carly said cheerfully.

*

Carly called Chet at noon Sunday. "I've got to see you. Can we go for a walk or something?" she asked.

"Can't today. We're on our way out. Going to visit my mother's folks. I'll see you in school tomorrow."

"Please," she said. "Won't you be back this evening?"

"What's so important?" he asked.

"I just need to talk to you."

Reluctantly, he agreed to call her when he got back, but it was after dinner when he did. "I'll meet you by the deer stand," she said. "We can go for a walk."

"In the woods at night? You're crazy." He finally agreed to meet her anyway.

She wore her new red-and-blue ski parka for warmth and carried a flashlight to light her way under the trees where the full moon didn't reach. It was so dark she didn't see Chet until he asked, "So what's up?"

She could feel the hard little acorns from the oak tree underfoot. Treetops creaked eerily in the wind and squeaked when a leaning trunk rubbed against an-other. Strolling in the woods at night wasn't as good an idea as she'd thought. "Let's climb up to the stand," she said.

"This better be good," he told her and climbed the crosspieces quickly. She followed him, and they crouched side by side with their arms around their knees looking off into the clearing where the deer no longer seemed to come.

She flicked her flashlight off. "It's about my father," she said. "I want to tell you why I'm mad at him and hear what you think."

"Why do you care what I think?"

"Just listen. Please."

He sighed. "I'm listening."

The words flowed out smoothly, the whole saga of her mother's illness and her father's failure. ". . . Mother was so scared. She just wanted him to be near her, to show he cared about her by being home with her, and he wouldn't. He kept running away. The sicker she got, the more excuses he made not to spend time with her. *I* hated it too. It made me feel *awful* to watch her dying, but I stayed, and she was my mother and I was just a kid. If I could do it, why couldn't he?"

"I don't know," Chet said.

"Well, what do you think?" She socked his arm. "Don't you think he was cruel? Don't you think he was rotten and weak?"

"I don't know," he repeated stubbornly.

"Your father wouldn't have acted that way, would he?"

"'Everybody's different," Chet said.

"But if your father did act like that, what would you do?"

"Do you love him?"

"Yes," she said. "That's what makes it worse. I wish I didn't."

"So what do you want from him?"

"What do you mean? I want him to say he's sorry. I want him to admit he acted rotten and feel bad about it, at least. I want . . ."

"Then you'd forgive him?" Chet asked.

"No," she whispered and was silent as it came to her that what she really desired was for her father to be wonderful again.

Suddenly Chet grabbed her arm. He pointed down. The moon had found a tear in the clouds and was shining on the ground directly below the stand. She saw the doe, and then the fawns. Snuffling at the ground, the doe poked at the leaves with an impatient hoof. A few feet away, the fawns, bigger now, were rooting for something, nose to the ground too.

Carly's heart beat quickened. She thought she could see the fawns' spots in the moonlight. "Acorns," Chet put his mouth against her ear to whisper so that the sound wouldn't carry. "They love them."

Another doe arrived, as large as the first. The animal's ears swiveled, listening for danger. The first doe's head came up quickly. She snorted and with a flick of white tail was gone. An instant later the moonlight shone on the rumpled leaf strewn ground under the oak tree and nothing more.

"They heard us?" Carly asked.

"Or smelled us maybe. Nice though, to have them so close."

"Lovely," Carly said. She wondered at the lifting of her spirits. Chet hadn't given her any words of wisdom, hadn't kissed her or even said he liked her, but as she walked home through the woods, she felt peaceful. The deer had done it, her deer. They were still beautiful and free in the world and that was something good.

12

arly answered the phone. Her aunt and uncle were at work, and it could have been them or Megan or Chet calling, but it was her father.

"Hi," she said, on guard as soon as she heard his voice.

"Well, I finally caught you in," he began confidently. "You must be having a ball there with the cows and the chickens. Whenever I call, you're either out or busy."

"I've made some friends," she said. "How are you doing?"

"Not bad. I got your letter. Pretty decent letter for a change."

"Thanks."

"So I decided to make you an offer you can't refuse."

"Such as?"

"Well, you've got to be bored with all that backwoods peace and quiet by now. How about meeting me in New York for a big city Thanksgiving weekend?"

"I've got other plans."

"We could see the Macy's parade," he said as if he hadn't heard her. "Remember how we always meant to go to the Big Apple for it some day? We'll do up the town, take in a couple of shows. I'll finish my business before you come so nothing can get in the way of our time together."

His enthusiasm was seductive and so was the offer, but Carly managed to resist. "Thanks. That sounds nice, but I'm staying with Lu and Ben for Thanksgiving."

Then and there, Carly resigned herself to visiting Ben's family in the Berkshires. She'd confided to Megan that she didn't want to leave town for Thanksgiving, but Megan hadn't come through with an invitation, and fresh-killed venison at the Grahams', where an invitation would be easier to come by, was unthinkable.

Her father's silence lasted too long. Carly wondered if he was hurt, angry, or stumped. Finally he said, "Do you intend to stay mad at me the rest of your life?"

"I don't plan my feelings," she said.

"You know how you're making *me* feel, don't you?" he asked.

"Angry," she said. "You told me in your last letter."

She could hear his intake of breath. "Okay, so you don't care. You're a hard-hearted kid, but you're mine and I happen to love you. Don't you love me at all anymore, Carly?"

I do, she thought and clenched her teeth to keep from saying so. He was making her suffer too, but just because she was a kid and dependent on him didn't mean she was going to let him escape. He had treated Mother badly, and Carly was the only one to punish him for that, even if she had to punish herself at the same time.

The phone call set off another siege of the purple pain.

*

Gunshots cracked the air and echoed through the surrounding hills all week. Hunters were practicing their marksmanship for the opening day of the hunting season, which was Saturday.

Carly's skin crawled every time she heard a shot. She reread the signs she'd posted around the perimeters of Lu and Ben's land: "No hunting. No firearms. All violators are subject to legal penalties." The signs were beginning to seem like a very fragile defense. There was a fever in the local population. Every conversation Carly overheard in the convenience store or in school had to do with tagging a deer, and who was trying out a new muzzle loader, and who was going out for a trophy buck this year.

Chet joined her on the bus on the way home from school Wednesday and warned, "Don't go walking through the woods in deer hunting season. Those weekend hunters will shoot at anything that moves. You'd better wear bright red or orange outdoors for the next few weeks."

"Gross," she said in disgust.

"Yeah." He grinned as if he didn't really think so.

"You're going hunting with your father?"

"Sure I am. He's leading a drive for four other guys. We're gonna camp up by Long Pond for a few nights. I can't wait."

"I hope you don't catch anything."

"Now is that nice?" he asked.

"I'm sorry, but I just don't want you to come back with blood on your hands. Even if the deer do need to be weeded out, I'm positive shooting them is the wrong way to do it."

"Guess you're not going to want to have much to do with me until hunting season is over, huh?"

"You just better take care of my buck," she warned before she left him.

*

Ben had Thursday off. By three o'clock when Carly got home from school, he had cut down the dead hickory that had been leaning dangerously over the roof of the house. The yard was a mess of branches. "Need any help?" she asked.

"Sure." He gave her that approving smile she'd been winning from him regularly and set her to stacking logs on the woodpile. She heard the ping of a small caliber rifle and flinched automatically without thinking much about it. Her deer were safe until the weekend.

They were indoors discussing what to make for dinner when the phone call came. Ben answered. Carly was getting out the potatoes as she heard him say, "I see, yeah, I see. Yeah, I guess that's best. Okay, sure." It

144

was only when he'd hung up and stood there staring at her that she got scared.

"What's wrong?" she demanded. Her immediate fear was that something had happened to her father.

Ben looked unhappy. He shrugged. "That was Harry Graham. Seems someone accidentally shot a deer with a .22 and the animal's wandered into our land. He wanted permission to track it so he can finish it off instead of letting it bleed to death."

"But it's not deer hunting season yet."

"Right. Like he said, it was an accident."

"I bet! And how does he know the deer was really hurt if it got away? Let's go look for it and try to help it ourselves."

"Carly, it was a gut shot. That means the buck's suffering."

"Buck? Not my buck!"

"Maybe not. I mean, all Harry knows is that it had antlers, but— Listen, the best thing we can do right now is let Harry finish it off."

She raised her hands to her cheeks. "No," she said. "No, no, no!"

"Carly," Ben said gently. "I know how you feel, but it was an accident."

"You don't know how I feel," she screamed. "And anyway, it doesn't matter how I feel. My buck is all that matters."

She didn't stop to put on her winter jacket before she ran out the door. She tore across the yard to the ground where she had faithfully tossed out the apples. Nothing there. She listened, but all she could hear was her own breathing. Her breath made small clouds in the chill November air. The sound of another shot sent her racing into the woods in the direction of the deer stand.

Her buck hadn't made it that far. She saw Harry, rifle in hand, standing over a deer whose legs protruded from a thicket. When she drew up beside Harry, she saw the antlers, the elegant horns still handsome on the limp head. Already her buck's eyes were glazed. Blood oozed from the gunshot wounds and a trail of it led to the body. She didn't need Harry to tell her the animal was dead.

"It was an accident," Harry said. "Too bad."

"That's my buck," Carly screamed.

"It is? I'm sorry, honey. It's too bad," Harry repeated lamely.

She shrank away from him and ran without thinking. Her feet took her to the deer stand.

As soon as she got her breath back, she sat still as Chet had taught her to sit, listening. Branches shivered and creaked, and somewhere a woodpecker knocked monotonously on wood as it dug for insects. She heard no other bird sounds, no scuffle of small animals in the leaves, and it was getting dark. She imagined her buck staggering toward some thicket to escape the draining pain in his belly . . . then she saw her mother's eyes, large in her pale pinched face, and heard the whimper as she regained consciousness where the pain waited to possess her. She had felt so help-less watching Mother suffer—so full of guilt because she couldn't satisfy the longing in her mother's eyes or alleviate the pain. Her mother had suffered, and now it was Carly's turn.

"Come roller-skating with me," her friend Marcella had said one day. "Skip the hospital this afternoon. It's summer vacation, Carly. You can have a *little* fun, can't you?"

Tempting, especially since it had gotten harder every day for Carly to leave day camp at one and take a bus to the hospital where she'd been granted special visiting rights for her mother's sake. Every day Carly had to make herself walk down the tiled corridors past all the sick people with their tubes and their bed pans and Foley catheters, past the nurses' station in the center, into the last room on the left. There the shades were always drawn because the light hurt Mother's eyes. The cool green walls were full of shadows.

"Hi, Ma, I'm here." Smile, bend and lightly kiss the skeletal head. Sometimes a crinkle of smile in return, sometimes just a flash of pain or no response at all. She brought small gifts to please Mother. Sachet scent of lilac. "Doesn't it smell like spring, Ma?" Blue satin unicorn. "Feel how silky." Until it was useless and her mother's senses failed to give her even an instant of pleasure.

Her mother probably wouldn't even be aware she hadn't come, Carly had told herself that day with Marcella. Date and hour had lost their meaning in the hospital room. Besides, if Mother were conscious, she would *want* Carly to go out with her friends. So she'd gone, she and pretty Marcella with the long legs. And they'd met a couple of boys, and skated round the rink hand in hand with the boys for a couples' dance. Carly had laughed a lot and enjoyed her own healthy body which melded with the music that rose above the roar of the grinding skates. Fun, ordinary, regular everyday fun. It felt wonderful to enjoy life.

The next morning her father had come into her bedroom. He'd sat down on her bed and picked up her hand. Even before he said anything, she'd known.

"The hospital called, Carly. She's gone."

Her punishment for missing one day. All her months of devotion had been inadequate. She hadn't loved her mother enough when it counted. Her mother had had to die alone, deserted in the end not only by her husband, but by her daughter as well.

Her father had said very little about her mother's death except that it was good she wasn't suffering anymore. They had gone through the funeral proceedings stoically, side by side, but they hadn't comforted each other while the comforting words poured over them from friends and relatives.

The woods were dark now. Evening came early in November. Carly buried her cold nose between her knees and rocked on her heels, enclosing the purple pain which seemed to have become a permanent part of her.

She saw Chet come crashing through the woods with a flashlight. Then his head appeared at the level of the platform. "They're looking for you," he said. "You've got to go home."

"What are you doing with the buck?" she asked. "Are you going to eat him now?"

"Aw, come on Carly. Don't be like that. Pop says he'll do whatever you want with the body. . . . You want us to bury it?"

"What do I care now that he's dead."

"Look, I'm sorry. I thought he had a chance to make it through the season. I mean, nobody else knew his habits. So I thought—but it didn't work out."

"Who killed him?"

"I don't know."

"I bet it was Joe, and I hope he chokes to death on his own meanness."

"Come on down now," Chet said. "You're cold." He waited for her at the foot of the tree and wrapped her in his vest with the cutoff sleeves when she got down. "I'll walk you home," he said.

"Let's go to your house. I want to talk to Joe."

"Yell at him, you mean?"

"Oh, don't you think I should yell at him?" she asked sarcastically.

"Sure, if it'll make you feel better. I'll even punch him out if you want me to."

"You will?"

"Yeah, if that'll make you feel better."

She walked into the Grahams' warm kitchen which smelled of wood smoke. Harry was sitting across the table from Gladys, staring at the steam rising from his mug.

"Good. You found her," Harry said. "Better call your aunt and uncle, Carly. They've been worried sick about where you got to."

For the first time she realized how late it was. Seven o'clock by the Grahams' kitchen clock. "Where's Joe?" she asked.

"Joe? I guess he's typing up some college applications at the library. At least, that's where he said he was going after school."

"Did he have his gun with him when he left this morning?"

"Oh, that's what you think," Harry said. He sighed deeply.

"Joe's gun's on the rack," Gladys said mildly. "He don't take it to school with him."

"It wasn't Joe who shot your buck," Harry said, looking into his mug. "It was me."

Her first impulse was not to believe him. He had to be covering up for Joe. But why should he? "You?" she questioned. "Why?"

"It was an accident." Harry looked up at her and even through the thick glasses he wore, she could see his misery. "I was feeling low this afternoon. Took myself off to the woods with the boys' old .22 thinking I might get a rabbit or two for supper. Sat there on a log thinking how it is, how a man can hardly make a living around these parts no matter how enterprising he— Well, it made me jumpy. So then I heard a noise in the bushes and aimed the gun. I saw something furry and took a shot at it without thinking. Shouldn't have. If I hadn't been in such a foul mood—But anyway, I got him. He'd been lying down in there, watching me. And he leaped straight up and ran off."

Harry put his head in his hands. "I can't tell you how sorry I am, Carly. I know how partial you were to that buck."

She looked at Chet who was looking at his father with no expression at all on his face. Inside she felt the same lack of expression, the stunned emptiness of betrayal. She had respected Harry. She had believed he followed the rules. Once she had respected her father too and thought he was special.

"I'd better get back," she mumbled. Chet thrust the flashlight into her hand and she let herself out their

151

front door. Halfway home she realized she was still wrapped in Chet's sleeveless jacket, but she kept going. Now he'd understand how she felt about her father, she thought. Now he would.

13

Friday she woke up, closed her eyes and deliberately went back to sleep, but Lu's voice woke her again. "You're going to be late for school, Carly."

"I'm not going," she said.

"You feel that bad?" Lu asked.

"I don't feel anything, just tired."

Lu let her be, but later Carly got up to go to the bathroom, and there was her aunt down in the living room reading. Carly leaned on the railing and asked, "How come you're still home?"

"Ben and I decided you shouldn't be alone."

"That's crazy. I'm okay."

Lu looked up at her and smiled. "Want me to fix you a nice breakfast?"

Carly smiled back. "Okay."

"And then how about helping me make those pies I want to take to Ben's family? We can make them and freeze them."

"I guess so," Carly agreed without enthusiasm.

They didn't talk much, and not at all about the buck or the Grahams. Peeling apples for her serene aunt was somehow soothing, and the cider-sweet fragrance of baking pies lightened Carly's mood. By the time Chet appeared unexpectedly at their doorstep late that afternoon, Carly felt lively again.

"Hi," she greeted him and led him wordlessly to the living room. Lu was napping upstairs in her bedroom. "Did I miss much in school?"

"No. Same old stuff. Megan asked me if you were sick. She's gonna call you."

"Uh-huh." They sat down at opposite ends of the couch, and she waited to find out why he'd come.

"I wanted to tell you what we did with the buck," he said.

Immediately, she stiffened. "What did you do?"

"Well, we buried the head and cut up the meat and Pop gave it to a woman he knows who works at the old people's home."

"Ugh," she said, withdrawing into herself as her spirits plunged again.

"Hey," he said. "Isn't that better than wasting it?"

She looked at him wide-eyed, aware suddenly of how different her values were from his. He hadn't loved the buck. To him, it was just an animal, and a dead animal was only a piece of meat. "That doesn't excuse Harry— that he gave it away instead of eating it," she said.

"What's the matter with you?" Chet demanded. "You want Pop to turn himself in to the game warden? He feels bad enough to do it, but he can't afford to pay the fine. Why do you have to be so unreasonable? You really are nuts, you know?"

"And *you* don't care about right and wrong. Just because he's your father, whatever he does is okay," she accused.

"My father's a good man. And don't you forget it," Chet said. His eyes were blue laser beams burning into her. Impatiently, he stood up and stomped out of the house. The door slammed behind him.

"Well," Lu said as she came down the stairs, "I guess he told you off."

"He got mad," Carly observed.

"I'll say. What are you going to do about it?"

"Nothing."

Carly flicked on the television set and sat down in front of it, not to watch, but as a cover for her brooding. She didn't want to talk to Lu about Chet. Making him angry could mean the end of her friendship with him, but she didn't care about that. She didn't care about anything much just now. She was back in the bleak landscape she'd awakened to this morning.

Ben came home. He watched Carly pick at her dinner and pretend to eat. "Hunting season starts tomorrow," Ben said.

"I know," Carly said listlessly. For once Ben didn't pursue whatever instruction he had in mind to give her.

*

She returned to school on Monday, three days before Thanksgiving. Chet looked right through her and didn't say hello.

"You and Chet have a fight or something?" Megan asked her at lunchtime when he walked past them without a glance.

"He's mad at me."

"You got *Chet* mad? How did you do that?" Megan asked, but Carly didn't feel like explaining.

After a day of having Chet pretend she didn't exist, Carly decided she couldn't just chop him out of her life as if he'd never been in it. That kind of denial was childish. She waited outside the school and caught his arm as he loped by on his way to the buses and home. "I have to talk to you, Chet. Would you come over to the house? Please?"

"No," he said.

"But I need your help."

"About what?"

"I need to understand something."

He looked at her narrowly. "That's for sure," he said. And then, after a pause, "Maybe I'll come."

She thought he would. He always had.

All the way home she stared out the bus window mulling things over. That morning Ben had tried to convince her that Harry deserved credit for admitting his guilt and doing the best he could with the buck for her sake. "It's hard for a man like Harry to own up to a wrong act, Carly," Ben had said. "Harry's proud and a pretty decent guy."

"I could get the game warden after him and have him fined for what he did," Carly had reminded Ben. "It wasn't just a little thing."

"I guess you could if you were vindictive."

"I'm not, but I don't think Harry Graham's white-washed himself either."

Before Carly had left for school, Lu had asked her, "Feeling better, honey?"

"I'm okay, Lu. Don't worry about me."

"You don't sound good. . . . You're not still upset about the buck?"

"You think he was just a deer? Well, he was a lot more than that to me, and I don't care if that's crazy. It's how I feel," Carly had said. "I loved him and his family, and I was going to protect them, him especially. I just can't stand the way it all comes out."

"You mean dying?"

"Not just dying. The way we treat each other. The way we keep failing each other."

"Oh, Carly," Lu had said, "what can I say?"

"You don't have to say anything. . . . Really, Lu. I'm okay." She sent her aunt off to work with a hug and more assurances that all was well.

No one sat beside Carly on the bus going home. Chet was in the back with his friends, practicing wolf-whistles. The enraged bus driver finally threatened punishment for all his passengers because he couldn't locate the source of the annoying noises. Outside the gray-white sky also threatened. "It's gonna snow for sure," the kid in front of Carly told his seat partner.

Two hunters in their red jackets and billed caps with registration numbers prominently displayed were heading down into a ravine with rifles in their hands. They'd left their car illegally parked on a shoulder of the county road, and, to get around it, the bus driver had to pull into the oncoming traffic lane. Carly felt remote from the bus driver's ire, not excited about the first snow, not excited about anything anymore.

She let herself into the empty house and promptly began building up the fire in the stove as Ben had taught her, laying each piece of firewood in crosswise. A newspaper twist inserted below helped reignite the fire. She left the iron door open so that she could watch the flames. Then she made a pot of cocoa, set out some cookies on the coffee table, and waited for Chet.

Half an hour later she began to doubt that he was coming. She was sitting there with the purple pain throbbing in her chest when he finally knocked at the door.

She forced out a cheerful, "Hi." Snowflakes covered his hair and shoulders. Individual crystals the size of half dollars were landing like moths on tree branches and the browned-over grass. They made the world look unreal. Carly stared entranced for a few seconds, then recalled herself and stood aside to let Chet in.

He scuffed his work boots on the mat and hung his red wool shirt with the hunting license pinned to the pocket on a peg behind the door.

"That's my father's," Chet said. "He didn't want me walking through the woods without it. Those hunters from the city don't know where they are half the time, and they don't care whose land they're crossing."

She nodded, unimpressed with the familiar local complaint about visiting hunters, and offered him hot chocolate.

"Sure," he said.

She set two full mugs down next to the cookies. He took his usual seat at the end of the couch, and she took her end. She hadn't thought out what she would say to him, but she trusted that it would come to her and watched his face for a clue. As usual, his face concealed his thoughts, and his lips were firmly shut. She wondered if he was really as deep as she'd thought. She wondered if she'd been imagining Chet to be more than he was, just as she had imagined her father to be.

"So, how's the hunting going?" she asked.

"I don't know. I haven't been. Joe got a pronghorn Saturday, good size too. He's been still-hunting. That's when you go out alone and just track the deer. My father used to do it that way before people began badgering him to lead the drives."

"I thought you were going up to Long Pond with a group?"

"We're not going."

"Why not?"

"Pop still feels bad about the buck."

"Does he? Why?"

"Because he shot it. He said he didn't think he had it in him to be so careless."

"You forgave him easily," she accused. "You weren't even shocked by what he did."

"Sure I was," Chet said. "Pop's big on playing by the rules, and he thinks as much of those deer as you do. He respects them. You don't understand that, but it's true."

"You still admire him so much?"

"He's a good man. So what if he made a mistake. *Everybody* makes mistakes."

She nodded. Of course, she knew that everybody makes mistakes and nobody's perfect. "But if you love somebody because they're so wonderful and they don't turn out to be," she said, "don't you think you'd better stop loving them so much?"

He didn't respond.

"I mean," she persisted, "if they prove they're not worth it. . . . They could fail you again if you go on trusting them."

He grimaced and sipped his hot chocolate noisily, without embarrassment at the sounds he was making. She looked from his handsome face to the big hands

160

holding the cup. His knees were apexes for the steep triangles made by his legs. He was awkward and she didn't know why she liked him. "You really aren't mad at your father at all even though he betrayed everything," she said bitterly.

"What'd you ask me over to talk about?" he asked.

She was tempted to forget it. It was so hard, and she didn't want to drag it out again, especially if he was just the simple country boy he pretended to be. Despite her doubt, she heard her own voice begin low and heavy, "When my mother got sick, she needed love and attention from my father. Like, she'd beg him to go with her to the doctor. And at the beginning, when she just knew she had the cancer but she wasn't feeling too bad, he went."

"You told me all this," he said uneasily.

"Can't you listen again?"

"No," he said, and stood up as if he was going to leave on the instant. "It's between you and your father, Carly. Tell him."

She shook her head. "Please," she said. "If you think I should forgive him, if *you* think so, maybe I can."

Reluctantly, he sat back down, and looked at his knees. Her mind whirled with what she had to tell him and she caught at the first thought and began again. "My mother loved the theater. My father could have gotten season tickets, but he didn't. She wanted to go back to one special place in Hawaii where he'd proposed to her, and he promised her they'd go, but then she started hurting more and feeling sicker, and he began backing off. He couldn't find the time for Hawaii, and Saturdays he had to go into the office. The sicker she got, the less time he had. He was out on the golf course when she was walking around the house so weak that she could barely make it to the bathroom without falling down. She only had a few months. He could have made them happy months instead of leaving her alone and letting her feel he didn't really love her. Why didn't he?"

"Nobody wants to watch somebody dying," Chet said. "It'd make you feel helpless, and some people can't take feeling helpless."

"I don't care how hard it was for him. It wasn't going to kill him to please her. *She* was going to be dead, not him. He let her think he loved her and then when it mattered the most, he proved that he didn't. That's heartless."

"So maybe he feels bad about it and can't admit it."

"Who *cares* how he feels?" she objected passionately, and stopped because she was close to cracking.

He reached out a hand toward her and pulled it back. "Why do you want to keep making people over all the time?" he asked. "Why can't you just take them as they are?"

"Or leave them," she said. "I don't have to take them, I can leave them."

"Yeah, except who gets hurt by that? You or your father?"

She snorted. "I'll tell you something," she said. "I'm not innocent either. I'm not as bad as he is, but I did something. . . ."

He didn't encourage her to explain what she meant, but he was still sitting there listening; so she finished her confession. Her voice came out hoarse, as if the words had rusted inside her, but at least they were finally coming out. "You know what I did? On the last day she was alive? I played hooky from her hospital room. I was *roller-skating* while she was dying. I'd been there by her bedside every day for over a month, but that day I didn't go."

"She probably didn't even notice. I mean, if she was dying—"

"No, her eyes always brightened when I walked in the room. She noticed, even though she knew I was Daddy's girl, not hers. I mean, she knew I'd rather be with him and that I loved him better than her."

"You mad at your father or yourself?" Chet asked in genuine confusion.

"Both of us," she said.

"I sure wouldn't want to be you," he said.

"Why?"

"Because I don't see how you're going to get through life if you can't forgive people."

"But some things shouldn't be forgiven," she said. "It's wrong to forgive a mass murderer, isn't it? Forgiving makes it all right, and some things are *never* all right."

"And you're going to be the judge? Just like God, you're going to judge people and send them to Hell if you don't like what they've done?"

"So you do think I should forgive my father?"

"I feel sorry for you if you don't forgive him *and* yourself," he said.

The fire snapped. A spark flew onto the table. Chet slapped it out with the flat of his hand and shut the door to the stove. Carly sat there, exhausted. In the silence, a fine mesh of snow fell outside the windows.

"You have any more hot chocolate?" Chet asked.

She nodded. He asked if she wanted some too and took their cups to the stove behind the counter. When he came back, he ate a few cookies and asked if she'd baked them.

"Ben did." She held the cup he'd refilled for her without drinking any of it.

"They do a good job over at that Environmental Education Center, your aunt and him. They're nice people."

"Yes," she said.

"After Thanksgiving I'm going to be working with Pop, helping him cut wood. He's planning on earning some money selling cordwood this winter. . . . My brothers are all coming home for Thanksgiving. Our place will be a madhouse with babies all over the place. I don't know where everyone's going to sleep."

He was making conversation she realized and looked at him with surprise. He was trying to be kind. "I think I might go down to New York for Thanksgiving," she said.

She thought about her father. He was a selfish man, and he wouldn't own up to that or change. *She* could own up to her faults and change though. She could try to be more like the girl she'd pretended to be when she stuck by her mother that last year. At least, Carly thought, she'd respect that girl more than her old self-centered self. But what if she changed and Dad didn't? Well, they might not be as close as they used to be, but he was still her father and she couldn't help loving him.

"My father's going to be in New York at Thanksgiving," Carly told Chet, "and then, I guess, if—I guess I'll go home with him if we can get along."

Chet looked as startled as she felt at her decision. "You're going home to California?" he asked.

"Aren't you glad? It's the right thing to do, isn't it?"

"I guess."

Her lip quirked, and she couldn't resist teasing him a little, "Will you miss me?"

He didn't try to hide. "Maybe," he said, looking straight at her.

"If I come back for a visit next summer, will the fawns still be here, Chet?"

"Probably. But they won't be fawns. The button buck will have horns next summer, and the female, she could be big enough to mate next fall. . . . Hey, I hope you come back, Carly."

*

He really did like her, she thought later as she stood at the window and watched him disappearing into the woods. He'd admitted that he'd miss her, and he'd said he hoped she'd come back. He knew her well now, and he still liked her even if he did think she was a little crazy. Well, that was the kind of boy he was, sensitive and basically kind, the way his father was. And Chet had been straight with her, just as she'd expected him to be. . . . No, she wasn't God to set final judgments on people.

It would be afternoon in California now. Her father would still be at the office. She picked up the phone and tapped out his number, expecting his secretary to answer, but the voice was his.

"Dad? It's me," she said and waited out his surprise. "About Thanksgiving, is it too late to take you up on that offer?"

She heard his intake of breath before he said, "Carly, do you mean it?"

He sounded so happy. It felt good to make someone sound that happy. "I love you, Daddy," she said. "I can't help it. I still do."

"I was beginning to think you'd never forgive me," he said huskily.

"I'm going to try and forgive us both," she told him. For an instant, her mother's face came clearly to her, not wan with pain as it had been, but shining with love. Carly waited for the purple pain to well up then, but the place where it had been felt empty now, cleaned out and ready for the future.